COULD YOU ESCAPE A DESERTED ISLAND?

BY BLAKE HOENA

CAPSTONE PRESS

a capstone imprint

You Choose Books are published by Capstone Press
1710 Roe Crest Drive, North Mankato, Minnesota 56003
www.capstonepub.com

Library of Congress Cataloging-in-Publication Data
Names: Hoena, B. A., author.
Title: Could you escape a deserted island? : an interactive survival
  adventure / by Blake Hoena.
Description: North Mankato, Minnesota : Capstone Press, [2020] | Series: You
  choose: can you escape? | Summary: When an adventure at sea goes awry, the
  reader's choices determine if survival is possible for two friends
  marooned on a desert island with a deflated raft and few supplies.
Identifiers: LCCN 2019006000| ISBN 9781543573954 (hardcover) | ISBN
  9781543575606 (paperback) | ISBN 9781543573992 (ebook pdf)
Subjects: LCSH: Plot-your-own stories. | CYAC: Islands—Fiction. |
  Survival—Fiction. | Plot-your-own stories.
Classification: LCC PZ7.H67127 Cq 2020 | DDC [Fic]—dc23
LC record available at https://lccn.loc.gov/2019006000

Editorial Credits
Mari Bolte, editor; Bobbie Nuytten, designer; Eric Gohl, media researcher:
Laura Manthe, premedia specialist

Photo Credits
Alamy: Travelscape Images, 80; iStockphoto: Alfaproxima, 84; Shutterstock: Alex
Kosev, 104, Andreas Wolochow, 92, Arnain, 25, balounm, 46, BellaNiko, 28, Dmitry
Sedakov, 77, frees, 4, Gabriela Insuratelu, 42, hanohiki, 69, Jack Nevitt, 63, Jag_cz,
10, kanvag, cover, back cover, Kira Volkov, 103, Lee Prince, 57, lidialongobardi77, 97,
Peter Turner Photography, 98, pics721, 35, Shane Gross, 14, Shchekoldin Mikhail, 19,
Sony Herdiana, 53, Space-kraft, 39, Sunny Forest, 89, Vixit, 6

Printed and bound in China. PO4940

TABLE OF CONTENTS

WHICH DESTINATION WILL YOU CHOOSE?

Map Key:

1. Atlantic Ocean
2. Caribbean
3. Bahamas
4. Iceland
5. Pacific Ocean
6. Aleutian Islands
7. Indonesia (Java)
8. Australia
9. Coral Sea
10. Cook Islands

ABOUT YOUR ADVENTURE

YOU are about to go on the adventure of a lifetime. The ocean is calling, and you've decided to answer. Will you sail the north Atlantic and see rocky cliffs and icy glaciers? Will you explore the Pacific Ocean and play in the warm sun and gentle waves? Or is a trip to the great Land of Down Under in your future? But don't get too excited—you're about to be grounded on an island that only you can escape.

Every decision you make can lead you toward success or crushing failure. Make the right choice and survive. One wrong choice can mean injury, death, or the risk of never being rescued. YOU CHOOSE how your adventure ends. Pick wisely!

Turn the page to begin your adventure.

Chapter 1

SETTING OFF ON AN ADVENTURE

You have always wanted to travel overseas, and now you get that chance! You have been invited to go on a once-in-a-lifetime nature adventure. It's a great opportunity to view some of the world's most remote and exotic places, and observe wild animals in their natural habitats. What an exciting opportunity!

But before you start packing for your excursion, you need to choose a destination. There are countless places around the globe to explore. What interests you? Where will you go? What will you see? There are so many choices!

Turn the page.

You could sail the Atlantic. Northern Europe, with its countless fjords and many cultures, is just on the other side of the ocean. You would be able to see and explore places you've only read about in textbooks.

You could go island hopping in the Caribbean and visit sea turtle nesting grounds and enjoy warm, sandy beaches.

The Pacific has many exciting possibilities. Cruising the northern parts of the ocean to see glaciers and go whale watching would be an amazing experience. You'd be like an explorer out of a history book, breaking through the ice for the first time.

But southeastern Asia has numerous islands overflowing with different cultures. It is also home to some of the rarest animals on Earth.

The Great Barrier Reef and Marae Moana are two of the largest wildlife sanctuaries in the world. Both destinations are near Australia and can be reached by either boat or seaplane. Either place would be an adventure just getting there.

Which of the following adventures will you choose?

To sail across the Atlantic, turn to page 11.
To cruise the Pacific on a passenger ship, turn to page 47.
To fly to an Australian destination, turn to page 81.

Chapter 2

SAILING THE ATLANTIC OCEAN

Exploring the Atlantic sounds like the perfect adventure, you think as you enter the harbor. Your friend, Sam, and his dad wave to you.

They introduce you to the man leading your trip, Cap'n Bill. His ship, the *Moira*, is a 35-foot sloop. Aboard a small boat, you'll be able to get to out-of-the-way places.

Cap'n Bill shows you to the ship's galley. It is a cramped little room, but there is a cookstove, a sink, and a table for you all to sit around. Bunks and a bathroom are in the far back of the cabin.

"I've sailed this boat myself, to all parts of the Atlantic," Cap'n Bill says. "But it will be nice to have a crew on this voyage."

Turn the page.

He means you, Sam, and Sam's dad. As part of your adventure, you will get to learn the ins and outs of sailing.

Cap'n Bill pulls out a chart of the ocean and spreads it across the table.

"Before I can ready the boat," he says, "I need to know where you'd like to venture."

Sam leans over the map with you.

"What do you think?" his dad asks.

"We could sail south, somewhere warm, like the Caribbean," Sam says. "Or we could go north. Maybe head to Iceland, where there are active volcanos."

Both places sound like a lot of fun, but which destination would you prefer?

To get some sun, go to page 13.
To explore the north, turn to page 18.

"Let's go somewhere warm," you say. "We can hit the beaches."

"Only if we can go snorkeling while we're there," your friend says. "Maybe we'll see some sea turtles or stingrays."

After prepping his boat and gathering the needed supplies, Cap'n Bill is ready to set sail. You head southwest, along the coast of the United States. The shoreline stretches out to starboard.

During the trip, Cap'n Bill teaches you all there is to know about the *Moira*. He starts with port and starboard (left and right). That's the easiest part. How to rig sails and tie sailing knots takes some practice. Chart reading and navigation are even harder. You also learn important sailboat tips, like wearing a life vest and keeping yourself tethered to a safety line in rough seas.

Turn the page.

After reaching Florida, you sail southeast, skirting along the Bahamas.

"If you want to see sea turtles," Cap'n Bill says, "we can visit a turtle sanctuary."

You can't wait!

Four of the world's seven species of sea turtle live in the Bahamas.

But the ocean has other ideas. One night, you wake as the rocking of the boat nearly dumps you out of your bunk. You go above deck to see what's happening.

Lightning crackles across the sky. Thunder booms. Waves slam against the Moira's hull. Gusts of wind whip the sails about.

Cap'n Bill and Sam's dad are struggling with the rigging. You strap on a life vest and rush over to help.

"Don't forget your tether!" Cap'n Bill shouts. But his warning comes too late.

A huge wave washes over the deck. Sam's dad loses his footing, but his tether is clipped to the boat's safety lines. It keeps him from going overboard.

Turn the page.

You're not so lucky. As you reach for your tether, the wave sweeps your feet out from under you. You are tossed into the roiling sea.

Water surrounds you. You pull the chords on your life vest and it inflates.

In the dark, you hear Cap'n Bill shout your name. But you have no idea where he is. Heavy rain blinds you. Currents spin you about until you're dizzy.

You struggle against the waves, trying to keep your head above the water. You pass out from exhaustion sometime in the middle of the night.

When you wake, you are lying face down in the sand. You are wet and sore, and you have no idea where you are. But at least you are alive, and the warm sun is high in the sky and drying out your clothing.

Glancing up and down the beach, you see debris strewn about. You don't know if it's from the *Moira* or if Sam and his dad are safe.

Do you go looking to see if anyone else washed up on the island, or do you check out the debris littering the shore?

To look for other members of your crew, turn to page 22.
To check out the debris on the beach, turn to page 24.

"I've never seen an active volcano before," you say. "And how cool would it be to see one somewhere cold?"

"Agreed!" says Sam.

"Then it's settled," his dad says. "We'll travel the North Atlantic."

For a time, you sail northeast, along the coast of Canada. To port, you often see the shoreline stretching out along the horizon. But after making a stop in St. John's, on Newfoundland, you head north, across open ocean.

You sail to the southern tip of Greenland. The coastline is riddled with fjords, offering stunning scenery. These narrow inlets cut between the country's high cliffs. Even in summer, snow tops the mountain peaks. Miniature icebergs float in the water. "Bergy bits," Cap'n Bill calls them.

"Hope we don't hit a big one, like the *Titanic*," Sam jokes.

"Shh," you say.

Your journey takes you east, toward Iceland.

On your way there, you are caught in a storm. Winds whip at the sails, and waves rock the boat. Cap'n Bill has you go below deck to wait it out. But in the middle of the night, you hear a loud thud. A shudder shivers its way through the hull.

Turn the page.

Small icebergs are called bergy bits. Smaller chunks of ice are known as growlers. Larger pieces of ice are floebergs.

"Did we hit something?" Sam asks.

What happens next is a blur. Water starts flooding into the cabin.

Cap'n Bill shouts into the radio.

Sam's dad prepares the inflatable life raft.

Winds howl, and waves wash over the deck. You can hardly see as rain beats down on you. The boat sways back and forth violently.

In the chaos, you lose track of what's happening. You and Sam make it to the life raft, but you have no idea what happened to Sam's dad or Cap'n Bill. You wrap a rope from the raft around your wrist and hang on as best you can.

The next thing you know, it's morning. You find yourself lying in the raft. You've washed up onto a rocky beach. Sam sleeps next to you.

You are wet and shivering from the cold. Sam stirs as you get up.

"Where are we?" he asks.

"I dunno," you say with a shrug.

In front of you is a rough sea. Behind you is a steep rise up to a thick forest.

"Is the raft leaking?" Sam asks.

Looking down, you notice that it is not as inflated as it once was. That is when you realize you have little time to waste. You are in a cold, harsh environment. Your only way of escaping has been damaged.

What do you do?

To try to fix the raft, turn to page 26.
To try to build a fire, turn to page 29.

You are worried something might have happened to the *Moira* in the storm last night. Secretly, you are hoping someone else is on the island. You go in search of them. You do not want to try surviving on your own.

An expanse of bright blue sea stretches out in front of you. Inland, grasses, shrubs, and a few palm trees fill the horizon.

You turn to follow the beach. As you start around the island, you can tell it is not very big. The beach slowly circles to your right. But there are no signs of other people. And the farther you walk, the less debris you see.

While last night's storm was bad, your carelessness is the reason you wound up on this island. Everyone else is likely safe. It is probably best that you worry about yourself.

The sun is bright, and walking through the sand is harder than you thought. You're starting to sweat. That is when you look back inland and see trees and shade.

Hunger and thirst are starting to gnaw at you. You have not eaten since yesterday. You can't remember the last time you had a sip of water. There are probably coconuts up in the palm trees. But you do not know if there will be fresh water anywhere on a small island like this.

What do you search for first?

To search the ground for fresh water, turn to page 30.
To search up in the trees for food, turn to page 33.

Before running off to explore, you want to check out the debris. Hopefully you can tell whether or not it is from the *Moira*, and if anyone else may have washed up on the island.

There's not as much useful debris as you thought there would be. There are plastic bottles all over. You could store water in those. You also see pieces of driftwood. But almost everything else is just trash. While there are more items strewn about, none of it really looks like it came from the *Moira*. Seeing so much junk washed up on shore makes you sad.

Sam, his dad, and Cap'n Bill are probably all safe aboard the sailboat. Hopefully they have the Coast Guard looking for you.

It is estimated that around 8 million tons (7.3 metric tons) of plastic ends up in the ocean every year.

While standing there, your stomach rumbles. You have not eaten since yesterday. You saw coconuts in some trees that you could eat. But you also know that you need to work on a signal for rescuers to find you.

To search the island for food, turn to page 33.
To work on a signal for help, turn to page 38.

25

The raft got you here. Maybe it can aid in your escape. At the very least you could use it to sail around the island and hopefully find other people. Even small islands have lighthouses or other buildings you can use for shelter.

"We need the raft to survive," you say to Sam. "We'd better fix it."

Working together, you are able to pinpoint a small puncture. While exploring, you find an emergency pack. Digging through the pack, you find food and water. Some flares and a first aid kit are found in one of the pockets. There is also a patch kit. You are in luck!

You set to work, but quickly you begin to struggle. You have difficulty opening the patch kit. And then you keep dropping things. It is as if your fingers do not want to do what you are telling them to.

Sam tries to help, but he struggles too.

"I just can't stop shivering," he says between chattering teeth.

Your clothes are still wet, and every breeze seems to chill your bones. But you continue to work. Or at least you try.

What you do not realize is that hypothermia is setting in. It is getting difficult for you and Sam to think clearly. Both of you also find it tough to use your hands. When Sam stands to stretch his legs, he almost topples over.

When you finally realize how cold you are, it is too late. You find matches in the emergency pack, but you are shaking too much to light one. Several are wasted as you clumsily drop them onto the ground. You also don't have the strength to gather firewood.

Turn the page.

Greenland's Arctic climate means temperatures rarely reach above 50 degrees Fahrenheit (10 degrees Celsius).

You and Sam huddle together for warmth, but nothing can stop the uncontrollable shivering. First your friend, and then you, lose consciousness, never to wake again.

THE END

To follow another path, turn to page 9.
To learn more about survival situations, turn to page 99.

You are wet and cold, and you see that Sam is shivering. You realize that you need to dry out your clothes and get warm.

You look into the raft. There is an emergency pack, and you dig through it. Among the supplies you find food, water, and waterproof matches.

You and Sam then climb up to the forest and scrounge around for fallen branches and dry leaves. Both of you are shivering uncontrollably by the time you get a fire started. It is good that you got it going when you did.

Once your clothes are dry, you begin to worry about what you need to do next. You have food and water, but only enough to last a few days. You could go in search of rescue, or you could work on signaling for help.

To signal for help, turn to page 32.
To search for help, turn to page 35.

You know that you can survive many days without food. But water is another story. You have been out in the salty ocean, and now under the hot sun. Your throat is dry. Water is the most important thing to find.

There is a lot of vegetation growing out of the island's sandy soil. There must be water somewhere. But no matter how hard you look, you can't find any source of water.

By midday, the heat is unbearable. You rest in the shade of a palm tree.

That is when you see the green shell of a coconut hidden under some grass. You know there is food inside the shell. But what is more important is that there is also coconut water.

The coconut's outer shell is hard. You smack it against a tree until it cracks open. Immediately, sweet coconut water begins to leak from it. You lift the coconut above your head and let the clear liquid drip into your mouth.

Afterward, you finish breaking the coconut open and dig out the meat. There is not much, but at least it makes you feel a little less hungry.

Refreshed, you are now set to take on the task of making a signal for help. You walk back to where you saw the debris earlier.

Turn to page 38.

You have no idea where you are. In one direction you have an expanse of ocean. In the other direction, you have the beach, which is edged by a steep, forested slope. Neither are ideal. You worry about traveling around in an unknown place.

"It is probably best to set up some sort of signal," you tell Sam. "Search crews could be looking for us."

"But what type of signal?" Sam asks.

The beach is littered with rocks. You could use them to spell something out. A plane flying overhead might see it. You are also on the edge of a forest. Maybe you could gather more wood for a signal fire in case a ship passes by.

To use the rocks to write a message, turn to page 41.
To gather wood for a signal fire, turn to page 44.

Your stomach grumbles again. Food first. You set to work looking for something to eat. You remember seeing palm trees with green coconuts.

You stand at the base of a tree. It is a long way up to the top, and there are no branches to help you climb.

You pick a tree and hug it with your arms. Then you push yourself up with your legs. It is difficult work. The tree's rough bark scratches your skin.

The sun continues to beat down on you. Between last night's struggle in the ocean, trekking around the sandy beach, and now this, you are exhausted. You are incredibly thirsty as well. Your mouth feels dry. You are quickly growing weak.

Turn the page.

Halfway up the tree, you lose your grip. You slip and fall back to the ground. Stars light up your vision as you crack your head against something hard.

For the next few hours, you fade in and out of consciousness. You are hurt and find it difficult to move. Your lips grow chapped from the heat of the sun. Where are you? Eventually, you close your eyes one last time.

THE END

To follow another path, turn to page 9.
To learn more about survival situations, turn to page 99.

You do not know if anyone heard Cap'n Bill's distress call. And even if they did, how would they know where you are? You are stranded on an island in the middle of a great big ocean. The odds of being found by random chance are slim. You need to find a way to get help on your own.

"Let's fix the raft," you tell Sam. "Maybe we can find help."

Turn the page.

The Artic contains 94 major islands and 36,469 minor islands over half a million square miles (1.4 million square kilometers).

"There are probably people living somewhere on this island," Sam says, agreeing with you.

You saw a patch kit and pump in the emergency kit. You and Sam get to work repairing the raft. When satisfied with your work, you stow all the supplies from the emergency pack in the raft.

You hope to row around until you find help. Even small islands have lighthouses to warn ships of their presence. You could seek shelter there. There is also the chance that a ship might cruise by.

You row out from shore. As you begin to circle the island, the rocky beach slowly changes to a jagged cliff rising high out of the water.

The sea gets more treacherous. Rolling waves toss the small raft about. Waves splash you with water, soaking your clothes again. It is hard to row, or to even keep the raft facing forward.

"Maybe we should turn back," Sam says.

You begin to wonder if that would be best.

But before you can make a decision, a large wave pushes the raft hard into a rocky column. You hear a loud whoosh as air escapes from a hole in the raft. The raft deflates, crumpling into the sea. You try to swim to shore, but the steep, slippery cliff offers you no way out of the water.

The waves slam your body into the cliff. You have no idea where Sam is. You try to hang on, but your strength wears out quickly. Your fingers slip. You sink beneath the waves and drown.

THE END

To follow another path, turn to page 9.
To learn more about survival situations, turn to page 99.

You take a closer look at the washed-up trash. A sticklike piece of driftwood catches your eye. A shiny piece of metal shines next to it in the sand.

These give you two ideas. The metal could act like a mirror. You could reflect the sun with it, flashing light in the direction of an approaching ship or plane. Maybe that would get someone's attention.

With the stick, you could write a message on the beach. While a flash from the mirror might get someone's attention, the message would let them know that they should stop.

You set to work. With the stick of driftwood, you write HELP in the sand as big as you can. Once done, you sit down in the shade of a palm tree and wait. And wait.

Sometime in the afternoon, the buzz of an airplane's engine wakes you from a nap. You run out to the beach and stand next to the letters in the sand.

A small propeller plane is off in the distance, and not flying too high up. But you're not sure if they have seen your message.

Turn the page.

The United States Coast Guard spends more than 20,000 hours every year on search and rescue missions. Rescuers are located along the coastlines, island territories, and major lakes.

You pull the piece of metal out of your pocket. You point its shiny side in the direction of the plane, trying to catch the sun.

You know it works when the plane changes direction and flies directly over the island.

"Hey, down here!" you shout at the top of your lungs. "Help! Help!"

The plane turns around and makes one more swoop over the island. All the while you are shouting and using the metal to signal the plane.

While you doubt the pilot could actually hear you, you are pretty sure they saw your signals.

Help will be on its way soon, and you will have survived your adventure.

THE END

To follow another path, turn to page 9.
To learn more about survival situations, turn to page 99.

You discuss your plan with Sam over lunch.

"If we used rocks," you say, "maybe we could write a message that would be seen from above."

"Like 'HELP'?" he asks. "Or 'Save our ship'?"

"Yeah," you nod. "'SOS' might be easier since it's only three letters."

You set to work. It's harder than you thought. The rocks are heavy. You constantly get wet from the spray of waves crashing onto shore. And you continuously have to take breaks to warm yourself.

At one point, the fire nearly goes out, so you and Sam decide to take turns. While one of you moves the rocks around, the other searches for wood to keep the fire going. Everything is fairly wet, so you create more smoke than fire.

Turn the page.

By the end of the day, you are sore and exhausted. Your nose and eyes burn from the smoke. But after all your hard work, the rescue message is spelled out. Then, after stoking the fire, you and Sam lay down to rest.

You wake with water lapping at your feet.

The difference between high tide and low tide can range from 1 to 40 feet (0.3 to 12.2 meters).

You sit up, horrified to find that the water has crept up to where you were sleeping. What's even worse, the rocks you spent all day moving are now underwater.

"Sam, get up," you shout to your friend, giving him a nudge.

"Wh-what's wrong?" he asks.

When he sees the tide has rolled in, he shouts in frustration.

"I guess we should work on the signal fire," you say. You don't know what else to do.

Turn to page 44.

"All the leaves and branches are wet," you tell him. "They create more smoke than fire."

"That'd be great for a signal," Sam says.

"We just need to build it farther from shore," you say, sighing.

The slope of the island is steep, and you are constantly climbing up and down for fuel. By late afternoon, you have gathered enough branches. You hope you can attract the attention of any ships or planes out searching for you.

Later that day, you hear the buzz of an engine in the distance.

As Sam lights the fire, you grab one of the signal flares from the emergency pack. Between the fire and the flare, you have a thick cloud of smoke rising into the air.

A powerboat cuts through the waves toward you. You are saved!

From the boat's captain, you learn that Sam's dad and Cap'n Bill are also safe. Soon you will see them again and be able to return home.

THE END

To follow another path, turn to page 9.
To learn more about survival situations, turn to page 99.

CRUISING THE PACIFIC OCEAN

Going on a cruise is totally your style. You might not get to visit as many different places, but it will be easier than sailing. You'll have more space to move about. There is a crew to run the ship and prepare your meals. You'll be able to observe your surroundings more fully.

Plus, it will be a super fun. Friends from school will also be going. It is a special class trip for students who are interested in studying the environment and wildlife.

One day, your teacher Mrs. Johnson asks students for suggestions about what to see.

Turn the page.

"We will be studying the wildlife around the Pacific Ocean," she begins. "We could either visit the northern part of the ocean, where we might get to see killer whales and visit glaciers. Or we could travel somewhere more southern, like Indonesia. There we could see some incredibly rare animals, like the Komodo dragon and the Sumatran rhino."

"What do you think?" your friend Jack asks, turning to you.

Both destinations sound thrilling to you. You have never seen killer whales or Komodo dragons outside a zoo. Where do you wish to go?

To cruise north, go to page 49.
To cruise south, turn to page 52.

"It'd be cool to come across of pod of orcas," you tell Jack.

"Or maybe some sea lions!" he agrees.

You vote. The majority of students select to visit the northern reaches of the ocean.

"Then it's settled," Mrs. Johnson says. "The weather in Alaska can be cold in early spring. Make sure to pack warm clothes!"

Your trip starts with a flight to Anchorage, Alaska. Next you take a train down to Seward, a small port town along the Gulf of Alaska. From there, you board your cruise ship. It's not exactly what you were expecting—there are no huge waterslides or onboard entertainment. It is a small ship, carrying less than 100 passengers. It leaves port and heads southwest along Alaska's coast. You sail toward the Aleutian Islands.

Turn the page.

Along the way, there are excursions you can take, like whale watching or helicopter rides over glaciers. You take advantage of as many of them as you can.

One day you sign up for a hiking excursion. Your view is beautiful, with a snow-covered mountain in the horizon. The coastline is a protected area for Stellar sea lions. You hope to catch a glimpse of some of the rare animals.

Somewhere in the middle of the hike, you and Jack wander away from the group. You were trying to get a better view of the scenery.

You get lost trying to find your way back to the ship. It is nearly dark when you find the dock. All the boats are gone.

"They left without us," you say, stunned. "Unbelievable."

"What are we going to do?" Jack asks.

You could wait where you are. Although it's cold, windy, and a little drizzly, people could easily find you. But there is no shelter. You might find better coverage in the nearby forest.

Which do you choose to do?

To stay near the shore, turn to page 56.
To find shelter inland, turn to page 58.

"Let's go somewhere warm," you suggest. "Then we could see all sorts of exotic animals, like orangutans or rhinos."

Mrs. Johnson asks the class to vote. "It's settled," she says. "We'll go to Indonesia."

After waiting several long months for your trip to start, you're finally on your way! The adventure starts with a long flight across the Pacific Ocean. You land in Singapore, an island on the southern tip of the Malay Peninsula. From there, you fly to Semarang, on the Indonesian island of Java.

The country of Indonesia is made up of thousands of islands. Java is one of the largest. There are several nature reserves to explore. You spend some time touring the island before embarking on your cruise.

The cruise ship is small. It holds less than 100 passengers. Instead of huge buffets and famous entertainers, it has a lecture lounge. Every day, you listen to naturalists tell you about the different animals you might see.

Turn the page.

Indonesia's 18,000 islands contain 10 percent of the world's plant species and 12 percent of all mammals.

The rest of the ship is just as cramped. You're sharing your tiny cabin with three of your classmates. When the weather is nice, you like to take walks on the deck. The cool air helps you feel less claustrophobic.

One night, you think you hear splashing in the water. You lean over the railing to see what it is. But you lean too far. SPLASH! You're overboard.

You yell for help, but nobody hears you. You try to reach out for a rope or a handhold, but the sides of the ship are smooth. There's nothing to grab. The ship glides past you, and then gets farther and farther away.

Throughout the night, you struggle against the waves and the current. Your only goal is to stay afloat. You have no idea where you are.

At some point, you pass out from exhaustion. When you come to, you are surprised to find yourself lying face down in the sand. Somehow you floated to the shore of an island.

You have no idea where you are, or what dangers might be at hand. But you do know that you will need water, and possibly shelter and something to eat.

What do you do first?

To explore the island for food, water, and shelter, turn to page 60.

To evaluate your surroundings, turn to page 67.

You are sure people from the cruise ship will come back looking for you.

"Someone has to notice we are missing," you say. "They could be back at any time."

You do not want to stray from the shore, even though it's cold, windy, and wet.

You wait. And wait. As the sun sets, it gets even colder. While you dressed appropriately to be hiking around during the day, you did not prepare for the freezing nighttime temperatures.

If you had the right supplies, you could try to start a fire. But you don't, and everything is wet. Even if you knew what you were doing, you would never be able to get a fire going.

You are chilled to the bone. You can't seem to stop shaking. All you can do is huddle together with Jack for warmth.

Alaska's shoreline is more than 46,602 miles (75,000 kilometers) long.

"I hope they hurry up," Jack says between chattering teeth.

"Me too," you say.

You drift off to sleep only to wake moments later. This happens over and over again. But slowly exhaustion overcomes you. You close your eyes and never wake again.

THE END

To follow another path, turn to page 9.
To learn more about survival situations, turn to page 99.

You have no idea if anyone has noticed that you are missing, or when you might be rescued. You shiver.

"We need to find some sort of shelter," you tell Jack. "We're going to freeze out here."

Jack agrees. Your clothes weren't meant for sitting in the rain after dark. And since you assumed you would be safe on the boat by now, you did not bring any supplies. Your only hope is to shelter yourselves from the weather with what you can find.

You and Jack walk into the woods. It's not really any warmer there, but at least you have some protection from the biting wind and the chilling rain.

"Maybe if we can find some branches," you say, "we could make a small shelter."

Trekking around is tough because of the steep terrain. You are practically walking on the side of a mountain. After a while, you and Jack stop to take a breather.

You hear the crack of a stick breaking. You and Jack look at each other. Neither you nor Jack has moved. You peek around the tree to see what made the noise. To your surprise, there is a large brown bear lumbering in your direction.

You have heard that bears can attack if surprised or threatened. How will you get yourselves out of this situation?

To run away, turn to page 62.
To walk away calmly, turn to page 63.

You have not eaten since the day before, and you remember just picking at the dry sandwich in the dining room. You also can't remember the last time you had something to drink. So you feel like food and water need to be your priority.

You won't find any food on the shoreline. Inland, a steep mountain covered by a thick carpet of jungle faces you. You venture into it.

It is humid and hot between the trees. You struggle to work your way through the dense foliage. Plants are everywhere, but you are not sure which are edible. You hear birds, and there is a constant buzz of insects. You could eat the birds, but you have no way to catch them. And you're not about to eat bugs—not yet, anyway.

For now, you decide to focus on finding something to drink. There are plants all over. There must be water somewhere.

Listening carefully, you can hear running water. You search until you find a small stream that runs from the mountain above. You give the water a taste. It is cool and refreshing. Success! You take a bigger sip.

Right away you feel better about your situation. But that feeling quickly disappears when you remember you're lost. You don't even know how to get back to where you started. You have wandered around quite a lot to get here.

Maybe the stream will lead somewhere useful. But maybe you should play it safe and just go back the way you came. Which path do you take?

To follow the stream, turn to page 66.
To turn back the way you came, turn to page 69.

"Jack, there's a bear," you say softly.

"We have to get out of here," he says, his eyes wide with fear.

"I know," you reply. "So on the count of three, we are going to make a run for it. 1 . . . 2 . . . 3!" You both take off as fast as you can.

You hear a roar behind you. Heavy footfalls follow. They are louder with every step.

You dare to look back. The bear is almost upon you. Then you fall. You weren't looking where you were going, and you tripped over a root.

It's over. The bear's teeth sink into your flesh. The blinding pain is the last thing you feel.

THE END

To follow another path, turn to page 9.
To learn more about survival situations, turn to page 99.

You motion to Jack to look around the tree. His eyes go wide when he sees the huge bear.

"What are we going to do?" he asks.

"We're going to get up, and slowly back away," you tell him. "OK?"

You know if you run, the bear might think you are prey. And if your back is to it, you won't be able to see if the bear charges.

Turn the page.

Alaska is home to black bears, brown bears—which include grizzlys—and polar bears.

Jack nods, and you both stand. Then you slowly start walking backward, carefully watching where you're going.

"Talk to me, Jack," you say.

"About what?" he asks.

"Anything, just do it calmly," you reply. "We want the bear to know we're here and not threatening."

"Can I tell you how thirsty I am . . . and hungry . . . and cold?" he asks, stepping over a fallen log.

You see the bear off in the distance. It lifts its head at the sound of your voices. It sniffs the air. But it does not move toward you.

You keep backing away until the creature is no longer in sight.

Once you feel like you are far enough away, you breathe a sigh of relief. You go back to scrounging around for pine boughs to make a crude shelter.

"It won't be much," you tell Jack as you lean a couple branches against each other. You keep talking to make sure that if there are any other predators, they hear you.

"It just needs to keep us warm until someone arrives tomorrow," you continue.

"Do you really think they'll be back?" Jack asks.

"Mrs. Johnson will probably show up looking for our missing homework," you say.

"So," Jack says, "what are we doing with all these branches?"

To use all the pine boughs to make a windproof shelter, turn to page 71.

To use some pine boughs for the walls and some for a bed, turn to page 73.

Because of the thick jungle, you took a meandering path to find the water. You doubt you could retrace your steps even if you tried. You would probably just get more lost.

The stream flows downhill from a mountain in the center of the island. You believe it will eventually lead you to the ocean. And no matter what, it seems smart to keep the drinking water nearby.

The stream cuts a narrow path through the jungle. Bugs are still biting you and the forest floor is still thick and prickly, but it is easier going than before.

Still, you are exhausted by the time the stream leads you to a beach.

You take a moment to rest and think.

You're hungry, but you don't want to just rush off to look for food. You already know how easy it would be to get lost in the forest. And you don't know what else lives there. You will need to be careful.

You stretch out on the warm sand. The sun dries your clothes. At least you won't need a shelter to stay warm. But you could overheat. Although not the safest place, the jungle can at least offer shade and water.

Next, you dig through your pockets to see if you have anything useful. There's not much. All you have is some change, the nub of a pencil, some lint, and a soggy note from your friend Jack.

You're finally ready to get up and move. You poke around the beach and find some driftwood and a clear plastic water bottle.

Turn the page.

Your stomach growls again. It's harder to ignore. But you know you have to make your presence known on the island. By now your classmates will have noticed you're gone. There may already be people searching for you.

You use a stick of driftwood to write SOS in the sand in huge letters. Maybe a search plane could see that. But, you realize, a ship would not.

You look at the water bottle. It could be used to send a message. Then you look at the driftwood in your hand. Maybe building a big fire would be better.

To send a message in a bottle, turn to page 75.
To try to start a fire, turn to page 77.

You decide to go back the way you came. But it turns out that doing that is harder than you thought. You had wandered around looking for water. The thick vegetation makes walking in a straight line impossible. As you go, it only seems like you are getting more and more lost.

Turn the page.

It is important to pay attention and stay calm if you're lost in a jungle.

The more you walk, the more you sweat. Bugs bite your exposed skin. Vines and leaves scratch as you pass. You are thirsty again, and, even worse, you're hungry too.

Perhaps you should have stayed on the beach before rushing off into the jungle. You could have made a plan, or thought of a way to keep from getting lost. Maybe you could have found something to use to carry water.

You're too tired now. You don't have the survival skills you need for this island. You eventually manage to find the beach again. But you succumb to exhaustion and starvation long before help arrives to rescue you.

THE END

To follow another path, turn to page 9.
To learn more about survival situations, turn to page 99.

Your biggest worry is keeping the wind out. The chilly air seems to sap your body of all its heat and energy. You layer the pine boughs to make a round tent, with a small opening to crawl inside. You stack on as many as you can find.

Not bad, you think as you crawl in. For the most part, you don't feel the wind.

But as you lay down to sleep, you just can't keep yourself warm. The ground beneath you is hard and frozen, and there's no way to get away from it. Both you and Jack spend the night tossing and turning, trying to rotate which body parts are touching the ground.

Your memory of what happens next is a little foggy. You wake to frantic voices.

"They're suffering from hypothermia," one says. She sounds worried.

Turn the page.

"We'd better get them back to the boat," another says.

You are carried on stretchers back to the dock. From there, a boat takes you to the cruise ship.

The staff doctor on board gives you all his attention. After some rest, you begin to recover. But at the next port, Mrs. Johnson makes arrangements for you and Jack to return home. Your trip is over.

THE END

To follow another path, turn to page 9.
To learn more about survival situations, turn to page 99.

You and Jack lean pine boughs against each other to make a lean-to.

"Wait!" you say as Jack starts piling up more branches. He looks at you, confused.

"Feel the ground. It's frozen," you say. "If we lay directly on it, we'll still be cold, no matter how windproof our shelter is. We need the rest of the branches for a floor."

While your shelter is not warm and cozy, it is also not freezing cold. You are at least comfortable. You're both able to fall asleep.

The next morning, you wake to voices.

"Look, I see a shelter!" you hear Mrs. Johnson shout. "This way!"

Turn the page.

Your teachers and several members from the cruise ship help you out of your shelter. You are then led to a boat that will take you back to the ship. On the way, Mrs. Johnson grills you about what happened.

"I had to contact both of your parents to let them know what was going on," she says. "They've said you can continue on with the trip, but only if the ship's doctor says you are OK."

You know that when you get back to the cruise ship, all your friends will be interested to hear what happened to you. You will have an exciting survival story to tell. Wait until they hear about the bear!

THE END

To follow another path, turn to page 9.
To learn more about survival situations, turn to page 99.

In the movies, people put messages in a bottle. The ocean currents send them where they need to go. You know that's silly. But it also seems silly not to try. They have to work sometimes, right?

You dry out the note from Jack in the sun. Using the pencil nub, you write a short note on the blank side of the paper with your name and any travel details you can remember. You make the letters as dark as possible, in case they fade.

You stuff the note into the bottle and screw the cap back on. Then you toss the bottle out into the water. The waves slowly carry it away. It feels like hours before it disappears.

What you didn't think about is that you're in a foreign country. People do not always speak English. If people find your note, they may not be able to read it.

Turn the page.

Even if they can read your note, and even if they give it to the authorities, there is no way for anyone to know exactly where you are. You gave your takeoff and destination information, but in between those places are thousands of islands. It would take years to search them all.

Also, you think to yourself, *when was the last time you opened a bottle with trash inside?*

The realization that you have little chance of being found hits you hard. You never recover. For a few days, you're able to survive on water, bugs, and strange-tasting plants. But your will to live is gone. No one will find you for years. And by then, it's too late.

THE END

To follow another path, turn to page 9.
To learn more about survival situations, turn to page 99.

It sounds silly and hopeless to send a message in a bottle. A fire seems much more realistic.

But you have no supplies to make a fire. What you do have is a small piece of paper and some lint. You could dry them out to use them as tinder. And you should be able to find plenty of driftwood once you get things going.

Turn the page.

Being able to start a fire, with or without matches, is a lifesaving skill.

Having kindling and fuel is great. But what do you do without matches?

Your water bottle is clear. If you fill it up with water and place it in the sun, its curved surface would act like a magnifying glass. If you could concentrate the sunlight on the paper, maybe you could start a fire.

You use the pencil to draw a black spot on the paper. You learned in art class that dark colors absorb light. Then you set up everything in the bright sunlight.

As you wait, you organize. The lint is handy to feed the fire. You also gather some dead leaves and sticks.

It seems to take hours, and you almost give up hope. But when the sun is at its brightest, you get a whiff of smoke. The paper starts to blacken.

Slowly you feed lint into the smoking paper. When you see a small flicker of fire, you add the leaves and sticks.

You build up a bonfire there on the beach. Handfuls of wet leaves create smoke. A black cloud rises from the fire.

Rescue crews had been combing this part of the ocean all day. One of them happens to see your fire on the little island. They quickly land and find you.

As you're carried away by your rescuers, you watch your fire get smaller and smaller. Soon you will be able to rejoin your friends aboard the cruise ship. You will have an amazing tale to tell.

THE END

To follow another path, turn to page 9.
To learn more about survival situations, turn to page 99.

Chapter 4

A FLIGHT DOWN UNDER

Spring break is coming up. You're looking forward to lounging around and hanging out with your friends. But then your grandparents surprise you with a trip of a lifetime.

"Australia? Really?" you ask, amazed. You've been dreaming of seeing the ocean for years. And now you'll be visiting one of the most beautiful destinations in the world.

You struggle to contain your excitement. Finally, the day arrives. Your grandparents pick you up and take you to the airport. You've got a long flight to Sydney, Australia. Then you travel north, up the continent's eastern coast, to Brisbane.

Turn the page.

On the way, Grandma says, "Before visiting the Great Barrier Reef, we thought of flying over to Marae Moana."

Marae Moana is one of the newest marine parks in the world. It was established in 2017, and not a lot of people know about it yet. It sounds like a nice, low-key way to start your vacation.

The following day, you hop on a small plane. You fly east, over the Coral Sea and toward the Cook Islands.

High over the ocean, you feel a sharp jerk. An engine on the plane has stalled. The pilot announces that he will have to make a crash landing.

Where are we going to land? you wonder. All you see is blue.

What happens next is chaotic. Grandma grabs a life vest from under your seat. Grandpa helps you put it on. They assure you everything will be OK. You aren't sure you believe them. You hunch over in your seat, waiting for the plane's impact with the water.

You see stars upon impact. You hear a loud screeching sound. There is water everywhere. Your grandparents scream your name.

Then everything goes blank.

When you wake, you find that you are still strapped to your seat. Your grandma is helping your grandpa out of his seat. The side of his head is bleeding. There is a man across the aisle who is still buckled into his seat. You unhook yourself and then slide over to help him. He is groggy and limps heavily.

Turn the page.

You climb out of the plane. You were in the back half. The plane's tail is sitting in the water. A chunk of the plane's side is about 100 feet away, and partially sunk into the sandy beach.

"What happened to the rest of the plane?" you ask, looking around.

The risk of crash is higher in small, private planes than on commercial flights.

"I think it sunk," the man says.

You peer out toward the ocean, hoping to see the plane's rounded nose. But all you see is blue water stretching flat for miles and miles. There's nothing to see but ocean.

You have crash-landed somewhere in the Pacific Ocean. Later, you will take time to think about the other passengers. For now, you need to think about yourself and the people who are with you. What will you do to ensure your survival?

To gather all of the supplies you can find, turn to page 86.

To use the plane as a shelter, turn to page 88.

While Grandma tends to the injured men, you decide to gather supplies. You grab everything you can find, from bottles of water to seat cushions. You even find a lighter.

By that afternoon, you have a mound of items piled high up on the beach. You head back into the plane for one last sweep.

You set foot onto the plane and realize you were smart to take out as much stuff as you could. The tide is rolling in, and your weight is enough to make the plane's body gently shift back and forth. By the time you've finished your last inspection, water is starting to creep in. You hop out before your feet get too wet.

Looking at the pile of supplies, you know that you have enough food and water for only a few days. That doesn't give you long. You hope that the pilot was able to radio for help before the plane crashed.

"We should get settled before nightfall," Grandpa says.

"I want to find out where we are," the man you rescued adds.

To stay put, turn to page 91.
To explore the island, turn to page 93.

If you clear out the plane, you can use the body as a shelter. It will provide both shade from the sun and protection from the wind and rain.

While Grandma cares for Grandpa and the other man, you set to work. You pull out the chairs and anything that looks like junk. Any supplies you find, including carry-on bags, you toss in the back. You can sort through it later.

By midafternoon you are exhausted and sweating. It's hot. You decide it is best to take a break. You make a bed from the bags you've scavenged. Then you drift off to sleep.

Hours go by. You hear Grandma shouting your name, which wakes you. You thought she was shaking you. But she's still on the beach. You roll over to get up and find the bottom of the plane is wet.

Tropical storms can lead to extreme winds, flooding, and hurricanes.

While you slept, the tide came in. Large waves are rocking the plane. The sky outside is dark. Storm clouds are rolling toward you.

Some of the supplies you gathered are falling over the edge of the plane and into the water. You run after them. But the waves rushing around the airplane cause a rip current. You are swept off your feet and dragged into the water.

Turn the page.

As you fight the current, you crack your head, hard, against the plane's tail fin. You lose consciousness.

The two men are hurt, and unable to come to your rescue. Grandma tries to reach you, but the combination of the waves and the rocking plane are too much for her.

You drown, never knowing if your grandparents will be rescued.

THE END

To follow another path, turn to page 9.
To learn more about survival situations, turn to page 99.

The back half of the plane is partially submerged in water. It's useless as a shelter. But if a rescuer saw it, they would definitely come investigate.

You and Grandma help the injured men to the edge of the forest. At least there they have shade from the sun. While you're making sure they're comfortable, something catches your eye. It's a large, shiny piece of the plane floating in the waves.

"Maybe we can use it to signal for help!" you exclaim. Before Grandma can stop you, you're in the water.

You swim hard, avoiding debris and other things floating in the water. You don't want to think about those things. Finally, you reach the piece of plane. It's about the size of a kickboard. You grab hold and then take a moment to rest.

Turn the page.

In 2019 researchers discovered that shark attacks had increased over the past 55 years.

Suddenly, something hits you—hard. The metal from the plane slides across your hand, cutting your palm. Then you feel something rough brush your leg. A huge fin breaks the surface of the water. You panic and swim for shore as fast as you can.

The plane piece did make the perfect signal. Unfortunately, it signaled something deadly instead. You never make it back to shore.

THE END

To follow another path, turn to page 9.
To learn more about survival situations, turn to page 99.

You have no idea if anyone is even looking for you. It seems smart to get your bearings.

Before setting off to explore, you and Grandma get the two men under the shade of some palm trees. You want to make sure they are far enough away from the beach during high tide.

You've emptied the backpack you were using as a carry-on. Among the supplies you brought to keep yourself busy, you also brought an empty, reusable water bottle. That should be handy in case you find fresh water.

As you walk around, you see plenty of coconuts up in the palm trees. You try to climb one, but Grandma tells you to get down. You gather coconuts that have already fallen instead.

Turn the page.

You also gather a variety of plant leaves, flowers, and a strange greenish fruit. Some of them have to be edible.

When you get back to the beach, you use a rock to crack open a couple of the coconuts. You find a little coconut water in them, which you pour into the water bottle with mixed success. Then everyone shares the coconut meat.

You're still hungry. You try the flowers, and they're very bitter. You spread the rest of what you've collected out on the sand. The fruit has a rough skin that looks like large, green scales. The leaves look a little like lettuce—only shiny.

Which do you try to eat?

To eat the green fruit, go to page 95.
To eat the green leaves, turn to page 96.

You cut into the green fruit with a plastic knife you found on the plane. Then you take a small nibble.

"It kind of tastes like apple," you tell Grandma, handing the fruit to her.

She takes a bite. "It does," she agrees. "But I'd spit out the seeds, to be safe." You all share the rest of the fruit.

Between the supplies you found on the plane and the fruit in the forest, you have enough supplies to survive. One day, either a plane will fly overhead or a boat will sail by. By then you will have built a signal fire or written a message for help in the sand. You are confident that help will come soon.

THE END
To follow another path, turn to page 9.
To learn more about survival situations, turn to page 99.

You are not sure about the fruit. The skin looks like it would be hard to cut, and all you have is a plastic knife. The leaves seem like a quicker meal, and you're hungry. You roll one up and pop it in your mouth.

"Tastes kind of like dish soap," you tell Grandma, making a face.

"I think I will stick to coconuts for now," she replies, smiling back.

That was a good choice on her part. Not long after eating the leaves, you feel a cramp in your stomach. The cramps keep coming and each one is worse than the last. Your skin breaks out in a painful rash, and a fever sends both heat and chills through your body. The leaves were toxic, and while not deadly, they weaken you a lot.

The jungle is full of tropical fruits that can help you survive. However, there are also fruits and vegetables that may not be good for you.

Sick, you are unable to help gather more supplies. Gathering food is too much work for Grandma, especially in the hot sun. As your supplies run out, your party dies one by one from dehydration or starvation.

THE END

To follow another path, turn to page 9.
To learn more about survival situations, turn to page 99.

Chapter 5

THE RULE OF THREE

Most people who get stranded at sea are rescued within a day. The choices you make in that first 24 hours are crucial. A hastily made decision could make your chances of survival more difficult.

Before leaping into action, the first step is to assess your situation. What are the environment and weather like? Are there any immediate dangers you need to worry about? If not, then take an inventory of your supplies. Even things that seem useless could be helpful. For example, a torn-up shirt could be used to make a rope. A scrap of metal could be used as a cutting tool.

Once you have a clear idea of the situation you are in and the resources you have, then it is time to act.

The rule of three can guide you in determining your priorities. There are three basic things you need to survive: shelter, water, and food. Which is most important?

You can survive about 3 minutes without air or in icy water.

You can survive about 3 hours in harsh weather.

You can survive about 3 days without water.

You can survive about 3 weeks without food.

If you are stranded somewhere cold and wet, fire and shelter will probably be the most important. If your body temperature drops too low, there is a risk of hypothermia. This condition can affect both your physical and mental abilities to do even simple tasks.

When you set up your shelter, consider the location. A beach might seem the best place. It is clear and will give you a good view of the ocean. But in a tropical area, the beach can be hot and lead to dehydration. In cold areas, you will be exposed to to freezing water and high winds, which can make lighting a fire more difficult.

No matter the location, you can't forget the tides. If your shelter is too close to the water during low tide, it could get washed away later on. This is also true of any distress signals you may set up.

If you are in a more tropical location, fresh water might be your priority over shelter. Under normal circumstances, people can survive a few days without water. But that changes in places with intense heat, where you sweat a lot, or if you have to physically exert yourself. Dehydration can cause fatigue and dizziness, making it more difficult to complete tasks.

Searching for food is only something to consider once you have shelter and a source of fresh water. Most people are rescued before they even come close to the point of starvation. Finding food can also be a tiring task. Most animals are difficult to catch without the proper skills and equipment. You will also need a knife to clean them and a fire and tools to cook the meat. And it won't last long once you do cook it, so once it's gone you'll have to find more.

Finding shelter can be easy or hard,
depending on where you wash up.

Most islands have plenty of vegetation. But be wary of the plants you eat. Berries can be nutritious, but they also can be harmful. It is best not to eat them, especially white or yellow berries, unless you know for sure that they are safe. Do not risk eating mushrooms. They can be very toxic. It is also recommended to avoid plants with shiny leaves or those with leaves that come in groups of three. If you start eating a plant and it tastes bitter, spit it out.

Having and maintaining a survival kit is important when disaster strikes! What's in your kit will depend on what situation you might encounter.

There are many other useful skills you can learn for just-in-case situations. How to start a fire safely and effectively and how to use basic emergency supplies are good things to know. And having a survival pack on hand can never hurt. Remember the rule of three, and you'll start off on the right foot.

SURVIVAL SUCCESS STORIES

1704: Scottish sailor Alexander Selkirk had an argument with his ship's captain. The captain decided to leave him on an island off the coast of Chile. Selkirk had a musket, a hatchet, a knife, and little else. But he survived for more than four years on the island. He built a hut from trees and hunted goats for food and clothing. Today that island is known as Robinson Crusoe Island. Selkirk's survival story inspired the book by Daniel Defoe.

1914: The story of Ernest Shackleton and his crew is one of history's greatest survival stories. Shackleton set sail aboard the *Endurance*. He wanted to be the first person to cross Antarctica. But in January of 1915, his ship became trapped in the ice. Eventually it was crushed by ice floes and sank.

Shackleton and his crew dragged their lifeboats nearly 200 miles (322 kilometers) across an ice floe to open water. Then they rowed another 150 miles (241 km) to Elephant Island in the Southern Ocean. They suffered from frostbite, starvation, and thirst before being rescued in August 1916.

September 1921: Ada Blackjack, a native Alaskan woman, joined an expedition to Wrangel Island, which is north of Siberia. She was hired to serve as a cook and seamstress. The trip was supposed to last a year, but the team of four men only brought supplies for six months. Then the ship that was supposed to pick them up was unable to get through the packed ice around the island. One of the men fell ill.

The other men decided they would try to walk to Siberia to find help. They left Ada with the sick man. They were never seen again.

Ada cared for the sick man for six months until he died. She learned to hunt and build a boat. She learned to use the expedition's photography equipment and took some photos of herself in camp. She was rescued in August 1923.

1943: Future president John F. Kennedy was serving in the U.S. Navy during World War II. On August 1 an enemy ship rammed and sank his ship. He and the rest of the crew were able to swim to a small, uninhabited island.

Their food and fresh water lasted only a couple days. There was the added danger of being discovered by the enemy. Kennedy decided to explore some of the larger islands in the area. He met some natives who agreed to carry a message to nearby allies. Five days after their ship sank, Kennedy and the surviving members of his crew were rescued.

October 1952: Tom Neale dreamed of living on a deserted island. He got a ship to drop him off on an island called Suwarrow. He brought two cats and all the supplies he could find on short notice. Some buildings and animals had been left behind by previous residents.

Neale raised pigs and chickens and planted a garden. He lived on the island for 15 out of 25 years, leaving three times. He wrote a book about his life, called *An Island to Oneself*.

January 1971: Retired Navy officer and dairy farmer Dougal Robertson and his family set sail aboard the *Lucette*. They spent a year and a half traveling. But orca whales struck their boat near the Galapagos Islands. As the ship sank, the family crowded onto a 10-man inflatable life raft and a 10-foot (3-meter) dinghy called the *Ednamair*. Eventually the life raft sank and they were all forced to board the *Ednamair*.

Food and water ran out after a week. They collected rainwater to drink, and caught fish and hunted sea turtles to eat. The family was at sea for 38 days before they were found by a Japanese fishing boat. Dougal wrote a book called *Survive the Savage Sea* based on their experience.

November 2012: Fisherman Jose Alvarenga planned on a 30-hour fishing trip off the coast of Mexico. Ezequiel Cordoba joined him. Their trip began with bad weather that only got worse. A storm destroyed the ship's motor and global positioning system (GPS). Alvarenga used the radio to call for help, but the storm continued to grow. Then the radio died.

Alvarenga developed a way to catch fish without bait or fish hooks. The men ate jellyfish raw and drank their own urine to survive. Once they found a garbage bag full of old food, which helped keep them alive.

Cordoba died after two months. Alvarenga lived alone on his boat for another year before he floated past an island. He swam to shore and wandered through a jungle before finding help on January 30, 2014. He had traveled 5,500 miles (8,851 kilometers) across the sea.

OTHER PATHS TO EXPLORE

◈ When people are stranded alone for a long time, one thing they struggle with is loneliness. Survivalists suggest making a "friend" in order to have something to talk to. Go back and read through one of the chapters, but as you make your choices, make a friend. It could be something inanimate, like a coconut, or a bird you see fluttering around your shelter. Imagine having a conversation with your friend about each of your choices. How does that help you decide what to do?

◈ There are thousands of uninhabited islands around the world. Many of them were created by volcanic eruptions. Imagine you were stranded on an island that had an active volcano. How might that change your priorities?

◈ Even some of the smallest, most remote islands have inhabitants. What if you were stranded on an island with people who spoke a different language, had an unfamiliar culture, ate food you had never tried, and did not have everyday technology like smartphones or computers? What sort of choices would you have to make? How would you know if the natives were friendly, and how would you communicate with them?

READ MORE

Braun, Eric. *Fighting to Survive in the Wilderness: Terrifying True Stories.* North Mankato, MN: Capstone Press, 2020.

Loh-Hagan, Virginia. *Deserted Island Hacks.* Ann Arbor, MI: Cherry Lake Publishing, 2019.

Silverman, Buffy. *Surviving a Shipwreck: The Titanic.* Minneapolis: Lerner Publications, 2019.

INTERNET SITES

Build a Kit—Basic Survival Kit
https://www.ready.gov/build-a-kit

Survive Nature—Deserted Island
http://www.survivenature.com/island.php

INDEX

COULD YOU ESCAPE THE TOWER OF LONDON?

BY BLAKE HOENA

CAPSTONE PRESS
a capstone imprint

You Choose Books are published by Capstone Press
1710 Roe Crest Drive, North Mankato, Minnesota 56003
www.capstonepub.com

Library of Congress Cataloging-in-Publication Data
Names: Hoena, B. A., author.
Title: Could you escape the Tower of London? : an interactive survival
   adventure / by Blake Hoena.
Description: North Mankato, Minnesota : Capstone Press, [2020] | Series: You
   choose: can you escape? | Summary: Your survival depends on making the
   right choices at key moments when you are eager to escape from the Tower
   of London.
Identifiers: LCCN 2019008533| ISBN 9781543573930 (hardcover) | ISBN
   9781543575637 (paperback) | ISBN 9781543573978 (ebook pdf)
Subjects: LCSH: Plot-your-own stories. | CYAC: Survival—Fiction. |
   Escapes—Fiction. | Tower of London (London, England)—Fiction. | London
   (England)—History—Fiction. | Great Britain—History—Fiction |
   Plot-your-own stories.
Classification: LCC PZ7.H67127 Cs 2020 | DDC [Fic]—dc23
LC record available at https://lccn.loc.gov/2019008533

Editorial Credits
Mari Bolte, editor; Bobbie Nuytten, designer; Eric Gohl, media researcher:
Laura Manthe, premedia specialist

Photo Credits
Alamy: Chronicle, 53, Commission Air, 4, De Luan, 49, Hilary Morgan, 70, London
Images/Paul White, 19, Science History Images, 63, Stuart Robertson, 43, The Picture
Art Collection, 83; Newscom: Heritage Images/City of London: London Metropolitan
Archives, 30, 88, Universal Images Group/Dorling Kindersley, 24; Shutterstock:
Antoine Barthelemy, 58, Arndale, 76, Celso Diniz, 16, Dmitry Naumov, 104, Fedyaeva
Maria, 10, Jeff Whyte, 38, 100, Justin Delano, 6, Keiki, 35, Mistervlad, cover, back
cover, murtaza1112, 68; SuperStock: Interfoto, 97

All internet sites appearing in back matter were available and accurate when this book
was sent to press.

Printed and bound in China. PO4940

TABLE OF CONTENTS

TOWER OF LONDON

Map Key:

1 White Tower

2 Bloody Tower

3 Wakefield Tower

4 Byward Tower

5 Traitors' Gate

6 Beauchamp Tower

7 Cradle Tower

8 Tower Wharf

9 Coldharbour Gate

10 Jewel House

11 River Thames

ABOUT YOUR ADVENTURE

YOU are about to step foot into one of the most famous fortresses in the world. In the past, it has served as a home to kings and queens, the United Kingdom's Royal Mint, and even a zoo. It has kept vast collections of weapons, books, and even the Crown Jewels of the United Kingdom. And it has housed prisoners who spent the rest of their lives behind the walls of the Tower.

The choices you make will determine whether or not you become a prisoner yourself. Will you sneak past the prison guards to freedom or be trapped behind the Tower walls forever? You choose the path of your next adventure—or your next failure.

Turn the page to begin your adventure.

Chapter 1

THE FAMOUS PRISON

The Tower of London has a long history, and has served many purposes. First built as a stronghold for early monarchs, the Tower's walls helped them cement their rule over the land.

The central structure, the White Tower, is the oldest building. It stands at nearly 90 feet high and has walls 15 feet thick. It is one of the most famous castle keeps in the world.

An inner and outer wall frame the White Tower. Twenty other towers line the walls. Entrances in the walls and towers, called gates, allow visitors to move about the castle.

A large moat surrounds the outer wall. Throughout history, the moat has been filled with water from the River Thames.

Turn the page.

The Tower of London has served as a seat of power in the United Kingdom and been home to kings and queens. But it is most well known as a prison and place of torture. Starting as early as 1100, spies and traitors were locked up there.

No ruler is without enemies. There is always someone who wants to grab the power of the throne for themselves. But not every attempt can be successful. And after the dust has settled, the nobles who failed need a prison. As a royal castle, the Tower of London is the perfect location.

But traitorous royals and their supporters are not the only inmates. Corrupt government officials and thieves have been held there too. Trying to cheat or rob from the crown is a highly punishable crime.

Those who defy the church can also find themselves behind bars. These prisoners, called heretics, may suffer a horrible experience. They often have to endure painful torture.

The Tower of London is not a place where many would want to be sent. So why are you going? Are you a traitor to the crown? Are you being persecuted for your beliefs? Or are you headed there to visit a friend who is locked up?

If you are a traitor and spy, turn to page page 11.

If you are being persecuted for religious reasons, turn to page page 39.

If you plan to help a friend escape, turn to page page 71.

Chapter 2

A TRAITOR AND SPY

The death of a monarch could throw England into conflict. This was especially true if several people had strong claims to the crown.

In 1376, King Edward III was nearing the end of his life. But Edward's oldest son, known as the Black Prince, had died in June. The prince's son, Richard II, was next in line. He became king the following year when Edward III died.

But Edward III had other sons and grandsons. There were many who could rule England.

In 1399 one of those grandsons made his move. Henry IV forcibly took the throne from Richard II. This set in motion years of fighting between Edward III's descendants.

Turn the page.

Uprisings and rebellions began. Kings ascended to the throne, and kings were deposed.

In 1455, the War of the Roses begins. Henry VI's family, the Lancasters, descended from Edward III's third son, John of Gaunt, and are represented by a red rose. Edward IV's family, the Yorks, are descended from Edward III's fourth son, Edmund of Langley. They are represented by a white rose. The whole country is caught up in the conflict. Many people have to choose who to support and who to fight for—and that includes you.

Both royals are descendants of Edward III. Both have a strong claim to the throne. But who will you choose as your ruler?

If you are a noble supporting Edward IV, go to page 13.
If you are a spy for Henry VI, turn to page 17.

The Lancasters have held the throne for three generations. In 1461 Edward IV used force to take the crown from Henry IV's grandson, Henry VI. You quickly gave your support to the new king.

You were actually one of the few nobles to do so. But you felt that Henry VI was not a fit ruler. He surrounded himself with unpopular, power-hungry nobles, which caused great civil unrest among the people of England.

But now you are paying for that decision. Around ten years later, Henry VI took back the throne. You are labeled a traitor.

One night soldiers take you from your home. They lead you to a dock along the River Thames. You are placed in a boat. It takes you west, toward the Tower of London.

Turn the page.

The night is eerily quiet, except for the splash of the boat's oars in the water. You look up as it passes under the Tower Bridge. In the moonlight, you can just make out a row of spikes sticking up from the bridge. Each spike is topped with the head of someone Henry VI and his supporters accused of being a traitor.

You realize that you could also end up on the chopping block if you are not careful.

Your boat glides up to the Tower Wharf. The castle's outer wall looms ahead. You are taken inside through Traitors' Gate and handed over to a guard.

The guard leads you to a cell in the Beauchamp Tower. This is where you will stay until your fate is decided. This brick-and-stone tower is part of the castle's inner wall.

Because you are a noble, you have certain privileges. Your relatives or servants can send you food and drink. You can walk around the castle grounds under the supervision of your guard. You can also have visitors.

Your stay there should not be horrible. Yet, you are still unsure of your fate. You did oppose Henry VI, the current king. Your name is now tied to the word traitor. And as you saw up on the Tower Bridge, that alone could make you lose your head.

Maybe you could escape. As a noble, you can have your servants bring in anything you might need, including extra food and drink. You could invite the guards to share your treats to celebrate a special occasion. Then, when the guards are having fun, you could sneak out.

Turn the page.

Wealthy prisoners could bring servants and companions. Some royals were even allowed out for shopping trips or to go hunting.

Or maybe you could invite your friends who also supported Edward IV. And if all of your servants bring weapons in under the party food, you could fight your way out together.

To use the party to distract the guards, turn to page 20.
To use the party to arm your friends, turn to page 23.

You have worked for King Henry VI as a spy ever since the War of the Roses began. But despite all of your efforts, Edward IV still manages to take control of the throne in 1461.

This puts you in a dangerous position. You were spying against the person who is now king. You need to flee, or you could suffer persecution.

You make arrangements to leave the country. But before you are able to go, soldiers come to your home. They bind your hands and toss you into the bottom of a boat. You cannot see where you are being taken, but you know instinctively that you are headed for the Tower of London.

You are taken into the castle through the Traitors' Gate. From there, a guard leads you to a cell in the Beauchamp Tower.

Turn the page.

Your stay is not a difficult one, but you are not a favored prisoner. Most of the nobles under guard were also supporters of Henry VI. But the guards seem to pay more attention to them. It's not just because of status, though. It's because of their coin. They have plenty of gold to pay for their needs.

Most days, you are allowed to wander the castle grounds. Your captor is always following you. But following you all day is boring, and he does not pay much attention to what you are doing. If only he realized that what you were doing was thinking of a way to escape.

During your walks, you notice things that have been tossed aside as garbage. You find pieces of metal about the size of your hand. The guards pay you and your scraps no mind as you carry them back to your quarters.

The Tower, and the immediate land around it, covers an area of 18 acres (17.3 hectares).

You can think of two possible uses for them. You might be able to use their rough edges as a file to cut through the bars of your cell. Or you could scrape them against the stone block in your cell to sharpen them for weapons.

To use the pieces of metal as files, turn to page 26.
To use the pieces of metal as weapons, turn to page 29.

There are too many guards roaming the castle grounds for you to have a chance of forcing your way out of the Tower. You need to be sneakier.

The party's on. But instead of inviting friends, you invite as many guards as possible. Before you were imprisoned, you had a reputation as a legendary host. Before, the guards would never have been invited to such an event. Now, they'll be treated like royalty.

Your servants visit as often as they can. Fancy foods and drinks start to crowd your living quarters. It's costing a fortune, but if it helps you escape, it will be worth it.

On the day of the party, the head of your household staff arrives with one last delivery. One of the barrels of wine has a false bottom where a length of rope is coiled. You remove the rope and hide it beneath your clothing.

More than a dozen guards show up to the party. They are more than happy to get away from their posts for a little while. You have a table filled with delicacies waiting for them. You even hired a musician to entertain them.

There is laughing and joking. Stories are told. Music is played. The guards have their fill of food and drink. The noise gets louder and louder.

At the height of the party, you duck outside your cell door. You wait a moment to see if any of the guards follow you out. When none do, you decide that it's time to make your escape.

You exit Beauchamp Tower through doors that lead out onto the ramparts. Beauchamp Tower is part of the inner wall. You'll need to get off this tower and then find a way to escape the outer wall.

Turn the page.

You could tie the rope around one of the tower's battlements and climb down. Then you would need to head toward the Byward Tower Gate, which will lead you over the moat and out of the castle.

Another choice would be to walk along the ramparts all the way to the Traitors' Gate. From there, you could use the rope to lower yourself to the wharf.

To escape through the Byward Tower Gate, turn to page 31.
To escape by heading to the wharf, turn to page 33.

You invite some of your friends to your quarters and tell them your plan. They all think it's a great idea.

You set your plan in motion. You and your friends have servants bring food every day. You tell the guards it is for a party. You also throw in a bribe here or there. After a while, they get used to the servants coming and going with baskets of food. They never check underneath the food. If they did, they would find weapons hidden there.

You are surprised at how easy it is. But then, what makes the Tower of London impenetrable to attacks from the outside also makes it difficult to escape from the inside. Two walls surround the castle grounds. Beyond them is a moat nearly 100 feet wide. Armed guards are stationed at every exit. No one expects you to even try to break out.

Turn the page.

The night of the party comes. About a dozen friends arrive. You invite them in and then shut the door. When you're sure the guards suspect nothing, you open one of the wine barrels. Inside, you find swords and knives. Everyone takes a weapon.

"Are you ready?" you ask. A silent cheer from your allies is the answer you need.

Your personal guard is the first to succumb to your attack. Then you and your friends storm out of the tower. You easily overwhelm the single guard at its entrance.

Beauchamp Tower is shaped like a D. The curved part of the tower faces out.

Next, you head toward the Bloody Tower Gate. This gate will get you out of the castle's inner wall. But as you march across the castle grounds, you hear shouts of alarm. Then you see guards rushing toward you from all directions.

The clang of swords rings through the night air. You try to fight your way toward the exit. You want your freedom so badly. There's no way you can't succeed, you tell yourself. One by one, your friends are cut down around you.

Then you feel the bite of a sword. You scream in pain and collapse to the ground. Your attempt to escape has failed, and you won't be getting a second chance.

THE END

To follow another path, turn to page 9.
To learn more about the Tower of London, turn to page 101.

You think of making weapons out of the metal scraps. But would they really help? The small weapons would not be enough to take out so many guards. Plus, you really have nowhere to hide weapons in your cell.

As they are now, the pieces of metal look like junk. Your captors haven't given them a second glance. Mainly they think you are odd for keeping trash in your cell. But when you test the metal's rough edges on the metal bars of your window, you are happy to discover that they work well as files.

It will take you many days, maybe weeks, to actually cut through the bars. But that gives you time to work on the rest of your plan. You will also need a rope and a grappling hook to make your escape.

Using a rock, you're able to pound the other piece of metal into a hook shape. You only do it at night, using a blanket to muffle the noise. When you're done, you have a workable grappling hook.

During your walks, you pick up any piece of fabric or fiber that you can find. When the time comes for your escape, you will tie or twist them together to make a rope.

When you are finally ready to escape, you need to decide the route to take out of the castle. You could sneak over to the wharf and swim to the other side of the River Thames. But swimming isn't a very common skill. And getting across the River Thames would be difficult, even for an expert swimmer. The river has a strong current, and it is much wider and deeper than the moat.

Turn the page.

You could use the grappling hook and rope to get to the top of the other wall. Then you could climb down into the moat and swim across. The moat is shallower and much less dangerous. But the moat has its drawbacks too. Human waste from the people living at the castle is often dumped into the moat. It will be a smelly stretch of water to swim across.

To swim across the moat, turn to page 35.
To sneak toward the wharf, turn to page 37.

Having a weapon could be your first step to escape. At night, when there are no guards around, you sharpen one end of each of the metal pieces by scraping them against the stone walls of your cell. On the other end of each piece, you wrap strips of cloth to serve as a handle. When done, you have weapons similar to daggers.

One day, your guard takes you away to be questioned. Your captors want to know what information you have about Henry VI. You tell them as little as possible.

When you get back to your cell, you are shocked to see that the head of the guards has searched your belongings. He is holding one of your makeshift weapons.

"What did you plan on doing with this?" he asks, glaring.

Turn the page.

Byward Tower protects the main entrance to the Tower.

You simply shrug your shoulders.

He turns to your guard and says, "Do not let this one wander about anymore."

With that order, your hopes of escaping have been dashed. You are stuck in your cell until your captors decide your fate. Being a spy for a failed king, that could likely be a death by hanging.

THE END

To follow another path, turn to page 9.
To learn more about the Tower of London, turn to page 101.

Any guard leaving the party could come this way and see you walking on the ramparts. Climbing down and getting as far away as possible seems like the best idea. You quickly tie the rope around one of the battlements and lower yourself to the ground.

With your feet on solid ground, you stop for a moment to listen for danger. It sounds like your party guests are still having a good time. Everything else is quiet.

You creep along the stone walkway between the inner and outer walls. You hide in the shadows until you reach the Byward Tower Gate. Through this gate is the bridge that crosses the moat. It is your way out of the castle.

As you had hoped, there are no guards on duty. They are likely at your party.

Turn the page.

But your feeling of cleverness passes quickly when you discover that the guards locked the gate before leaving their posts. You cannot get it open. You cannot get out of the castle.

You are so close to making your escape. Without thinking, you let out a frustrated cry.

Before you can think of another plan, you hear the sounds of footsteps. Your outburst must have been louder than you realized! There is nowhere for you to go, and the guards soon find you. You are dragged back to your cell and locked inside.

Your plan to escape failed. The next day, you receive horrible news. You have been sentenced to be beheaded as a traitor. You will not have another chance to escape.

THE END

To follow another path, turn to page 9.
To learn more about the Tower of London, turn to page 101.

Your servant had hinted that he might be able to send a boat to wait for you tonight. The wharf seems like it has the most potential for success.

If you drop down from here, you would still have to get through the Byward Tower Gate. There could be guards stationed there. At this time of night, the gate might also be locked.

So you walk along the top of the tower wall toward the wharf. The night is quiet, other than the sounds of laughter coming from your cell.

Your plan to distract the guards is working. No one has noticed that you are gone. The guards who regularly patrol the wall aren't here either. They must be at the party too.

You make your way to Wakefield Tower without being seen. There is a walkway that attaches that tower to the top of Traitors' Gate.

Turn the page.

Once you reach the gate, you tie a rope around one of the battlements and climb down to the wharf.

"Over here," someone whispers.

You look to see friends sitting in a boat. You rush over to them and jump in. They row as fast and as quietly as they can. Every stroke carries you farther away from the prison.

You have escaped the Tower of London!

THE END

To follow another path, turn to page 9.
To learn more about the Tower of London, turn to page 101.

You're not confident enough in your swimming skill to risk the river. You'll just have to bear the filthy moat.

Once you have made a big enough opening in your cell window, you squeeze through. You then crawl over to the top of the inner wall. From there, you use your makeshift grappling hook and rope to lower yourself to the walkway between the inner and outer walls.

Turn the page.

One prisoner escaped the White Tower by climbing out a window and lowering himself to the ground with a rope.

With a yank of the rope, your hook comes loose. You walk over to the outer wall and toss the grappling hook. It catches on the top of the wall. It is a difficult climb. But you eventually reach the top of the other wall.

From there, you hook the rope to one of the battlements. You climb down, carefully lowering yourself into the smelly moat water.

The swim across is not easy. Slick waste coats your clothing. You struggle to breathe because of the stench. But it is a short swim.

After climbing out on the other side, you disappear into the night. You're free!

THE END

To follow another path, turn to page 9.
To learn more about the Tower of London, turn to page 101

The last thing you want to do is swim across the disgusting moat. The Tower Wharf seems like a cleaner, if more dangerous, escape route.

On the night of your escape, you finish cutting through the bars of your window. Then you use your rope to lower yourself to the ground.

Thankfully, there are few people about at night. You see some guards, but they are easy to dodge.

You reach the wharf and dive into the water. At first, swimming is easy. But soon you start to tire. The river's current seems to pull you in every direction. You make it about halfway across when your strength fails you. Your lungs fill with water as you gasp for air. The blackness of the water has you in its grasp. You take your last breath.

THE END

To follow another path, turn to page 9.
To learn more about the Tower of London, turn to page 101.

RELIGIOUS PERSECUTION

Religion has long played an important part in England's history. Even before the country was united under William the Conqueror, the Roman Catholic Church had made its presence known. The pope and the church's leaders have helped choose England's rulers and have influenced its laws many times.

But the church has become unpopular. Some people think the Roman Catholic Church gives Rome too much power over England. Others feel its leaders have grown rich from corruption. Church leaders collect large sums of taxes, and some of that money ends up in their pockets.

Turn the page.

On top of all that, church services are held in Latin. Most people cannot understand this ancient language. They do not even know what the priests are saying.

Fed up, people broke away from the Roman Catholic Church in the early 1500s. This movement was called the Reformation. A Christian branch of Protestants begins to form. Protestants do not believe the pope holds power over their rulers. They do not follow many of the Roman Catholic traditions. They also hold services in the languages that everyday people speak and understand.

The split from the Roman Catholic Church is not peaceful. Catholic and Protestant church leaders are often in conflict. Wars are fought and riots take place, all because of religious differences.

In England, the current ruler often determines which religion is accepted. Anyone practicing the wrong religion risks being labeled a heretic and is imprisoned.

You are one of those heretics. But who gave you that label, and what did you do? Which ruler will show you mercy—or take your head?

If Edward VI is king, turn to page 42.
If Mary I is queen, turn to page 46.

King Edward VI was crowned ruler of England in 1547. He was just 9 years old at the time. But what is most important is that he was raised Protestant. He is actually the first Protestant ruler of the country.

As a child, King Edward VI does not govern by himself. A regency council of English nobles guides the king's decisions and orders. They are all supporters of the Reformation. Not only does the council believe in breaking from the Roman Catholic Church, they have also created laws condemning many of its practices.

You do not support these rules. You believe people should not be restricted in how they voice their beliefs and opinions. This has put you at odds with those in power. Someone heard your words spoken aloud—and this is why you are being taken to the Tower of London.

Your guard leads you to a cell in the Cradle Tower. He will be the one watching over you while you are locked in the castle. He will bring you your food and see to your needs.

A dock stretches across the castle's now-dry wharf. It stands between the Cradle Tower (far) and the Well Tower (near).

Turn the page.

The tower you are in is part of the castle's outer wall. It faces south, toward the River Thames. The Tower Wharf lies between the outer wall and the river. Boats often dock there to bring prisoners to the castle.

Like most people condemned as heretics, your stay in the Tower is not a pleasant one. You are not given much time to get used to your surroundings before you are taken to be tortured.

A cruel-looking man binds your wrists in metal manacles. Then he has you step onto a wooden stool. The manacles are attached to a hook. The hook has been nailed to a wooden beam high above your head.

Once everything is set, your torturer kicks the stool out from under you. You are left hanging. The manacles dig painfully into your wrists. Your hands swell, and your fingers grow numb.

As you dangle there, your torturer asks you to give up the names of your friends.

"Who are they?" he growls.

If you provide the names of others who share your beliefs, the torture will end, he promises. If not, the pain will continue, and the torture will only get worse. That he also promises.

What do you do?

To end the torture, turn to page 49.
To refuse to speak, turn to page 52.

Queen Mary I was crowned ruler of England in 1553. She came to power shortly after her half brother, King Edward VI, died.

Even though they were siblings, there were big differences in how the two were raised. Edward was a Protestant. Under his rule, England broke away from the Roman Catholic Church.

But Mary is a Catholic. She wants her country to go back to following the church's traditions. She also wants to bring her country back under the pope's authority. She has called for the persecution of those who do not follow Roman Catholic traditions.

You and your friends do not support her. You feel people should be allowed to worship however they want. But you were too loud in your opinion. For this, you are labeled a heretic and are being imprisoned in the Tower of London.

You are locked in a cell in the Cradle Tower. It is part of the castle's outer wall. It faces south, toward the River Thames. A wharf lies between it and the river. Boats often dock there to bring in new prisoners.

Like other heretics imprisoned in the Tower, you are forced to endure severe punishment, including torture.

Your torturer is a bulky man who always scowls when he speaks. One day he lays you down on a device called a rack. Your arms are bound above your head. Your legs are tied down by ropes.

Then your torturer cranks on a wheel at the foot of the rack. It pulls the ropes tight. You feel them bite into your wrists and ankles. Your joints start to ache.

Turn the page.

"Let me know when you are ready to tell us the names of your heretic friends," the torturer says, pausing to give you a moment of rest.

Then he cranks on the wheel again. The ropes pull your arms and legs tight.

He cranks some more.

That is when the real pain begins. The muscles and tendons in your limbs are getting stretched beyond their limits. Your arm and leg bones feel like they are going to pop out of their sockets.

You could end it all if you provide the information that your torturer is asking for. If not, the torture will continue. What do you do?

To keep quiet, turn to page 52.
To end the torture, turn to page 54.

"I will talk," you groan.

The torturer unhooks your manacles, and you crumble to the cold stone floor. Your guard reappears with a chair and a small desk.

You are lifted onto the wooden stool. A well-dressed man who looks like a church leader enters. He sits down at the desk. He places a sheet of paper and writing tools in front of you.

Turn the page.

Stretching a victim's joints could dislocate, or even tear off, a person's limbs.

"I want you to write down the names of all your associates," he says.

You lift your manacled hands. But your fingers will not work right. You cannot hold the pen correctly.

"I can't," you say. "My fingers are numb."

"Then I will make the list for you," the man grunts.

He picks up the pen and starts writing down the names that you tell him.

When you are done, your guard removes the manacles. He helps you back to your cell, where you collapse on a bed of straw.

You are not put through any more torture. You are thankful for that. But you have just condemned people you know to a cruel fate.

Days later, you are released from the Tower. When you return home, you learn that all your friends and allies have either been captured or have fled the country. Some will suffer as you did. Others will be on the run for the rest of their lives. What you have done leads to many restless nights of sleep for you.

THE END

To follow another path, turn to page 9.
To learn more about the Tower of London, turn to page 101.

"I will tell you nothing," you growl.

You know that giving up the names of your friends will condemn them to this same fate. Some may be executed.

So you keep quiet. You endure the pain. At one point, you pass out.

Your torturer leaves you in a crumbled heap on the cold stone floor. Your guard manages to get you back to your cell.

You cannot fall asleep. Your whole body aches. Groans of agony seem to be the only sounds you can make.

You know that you cannot survive much more of this treatment. You need to escape. Maybe if you can contact your friends, you can find a way out of the Tower.

Lady Jane Grey was queen for nine days. She ruled after Edward VI and before Mary I. She was executed at the Tower on February 12, 1554.

But for that to happen, you will need help. The only two people you see consistently are your torturer and your guard. You have no other choice than to ask if one of them will aid you in getting a message to your friends. It seems like a crazy idea, but what else can you do?

Whose help do you seek?

To ask for help from your torturer, turn to page 56.
To ask for help from your guard, turn to page 58.

You hear a popping noise. Then your body burns with pain. "Stop! Stop!" you yell. "I will tell you all I know."

The torturer unties your wrists and ankles.

He and your guard fetch two chairs. They help you into one of the chairs. You have difficulty sitting upright, and they have to tie you to yours.

Moments later, another man enters the room. He is dressed in the robes of a church leader.

"I hear you are ready to speak," he says, sitting in the other chair.

You nod. You answer all of his questions, no matter how personal. You give him the names of your associates. You also confess to beliefs that oppose the Roman Catholic Church.

When you are done, you wait for relief. You expect to be taken back to your quarters and cared for. You do not expect what comes next.

"There will be no more torture," your confessor says. "But since you admit guilt, you will be burned at the stake as a heretic." He leaves without seeming to hear your cries.

You are taken back to your cell and put in chains. There, you stay until the day of your execution.

THE END

To follow another path, turn to page 9.
To learn more about the Tower of London, turn to page 101.

Your torturer sees how you are suffering. He knows the pain you are in and hears your cries of agony. Perhaps this will make him sympathetic to you.

One day as he is binding your wrists, you whisper, "You don't need to do this."

He says nothing. He continues his work without making eye contact.

"I have friends," you say. "Friends with money. A *lot* of money."

This gets his attention. He turns and stares you in the face.

"You think maybe you can bribe me?" he asks. "Then I'll be gentle with you?"

"No, no, I want you to help me escape," you whisper. "My friends will pay you generously."

He scoffs at that and binds your wrists extra tight. You wince in pain.

"If I did that," he says, "I'd end up right where you are now."

He does not show you any mercy.

You scream in agony.

Eventually the pain will be too much for you. Either you will die at the hands of your torturer or you will give up the names of your associates. No matter which happens, you are in for many long days of suffering.

THE END

To follow another path, turn to page 9.
To learn more about the Tower of London, turn to page 101.

You doubt your torturer would help you. After all, he is the one causing you all the pain. That is his job, and he is a professional.

But your guard might be kinder. It is actually common for guards to do favors for inmates. And it is his job to watch over you. He is the one who helps you back to your cell after you are tortured.

Prisoners were kept at the Tower between 1100 and 1941.

One night you ask him, "Could you take a message to my friends? I will pay you."

"I will," he agrees, nodding. "Just tell me what you need."

You will need paper and writing tools to send messages. But if you are going to hatch an escape plan, you do not want your guard reading what you write. Perhaps you could write secret messages, like a spy. You know the juice of an orange will produce clear ink. When heated, the letters will appear.

You could ask for a candle instead. You could use drops of heated wax to seal to your letters. If the letters arrived with their seals broken, your friends would know they had been read.

To ask for a candle, turn to page 60.
To ask for oranges, turn to page 62.

"Could you bring me some writing supplies?" you ask. "And a candle?"

"As long as you have the money to pay for it, I can get whatever you need," he says.

"That won't be a problem," you say, winking. Prisoners are allowed to have money to pay for the things they might need. You came in with plenty.

Once you have your supplies, you write a note to a trusted ally. In it, you mention ideas for an escape. Then you seal the letter with wax. You give the letter to your guard. You trust him not to break the seal.

The next day your guard enters your room. His superior follows behind. While your guard looks down at his feet, ashamed, the other man rummages through all of your things. He takes your writing supplies, any food you have, and all your money.

Then he turns to you. "Let's see you escape now!" he says triumphantly.

As he walks out of your cell, he turns to your guard. "I want this prisoner locked in chains at all times," he says.

"He saw the letter," your guard explains. "I had no choice but to let him read it."

He binds your wrists and ankles in heavy chains. You can hardly walk. And you are denied any contact with the outside. Now you have no hope of escape. You prepare to spend many days in the Tower enduring agonizing torture.

THE END

To follow another path, turn to page 9.
To learn more about the Tower of London, turn to page 101.

"I could use some writing supplies," you say, "and also a sack of oranges."

Your guard does not think twice about this request. As long as you have money, he can get anything you need—within reason.

You write a note with regular ink on one side of the paper. You ask for books to read and for news about your family. You leave small sketches around the edges of the paper. One of the sketches is of a candle. Hopefully your friends will understand what to do.

Once you have the oranges, you break one open. You eat half. Then you dip a sliver of wood into the other half. You use the wood like a pen to write a message with the fruit juice on the other side of the paper. In your secret message, you ask for an item to help you escape.

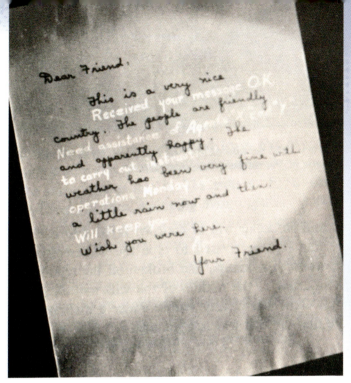

Spies have made invisible ink out of simple things such as orange or lemon juice, oatmeal and milk, and urine.

But what item will help you the most? You could use a weapon. With a dagger, you might be able to fight your way out of the castle. Or you could ask for a rope. You could use it to lower yourself down the outer wall of the castle.

To sneak in a rope, turn to page 64.
To sneak in a weapon, turn to page 67.

You doubt a weapon would really help you much. You would have to fight your way past your guard as well as any others patrolling the castle. They are all armed with pikes, which are sharp blades attached to long poles. You'd never get close enough to land an attack. You would do better to sneak away.

In your secret note, you ask for a rope. It arrives inside a hollowed-out loaf of bread, along with a message. Your friends will meet you in a boat at the Tower Wharf. You will just need to find a way to get there on the chosen night.

"It's so nice out," you say to the guard on the night of your escape. "Do you mind if I go for a walk along the walls?"

You slip him some coins. He nods and lets you go off alone.

The wall you walk along is known as a rampart. It is wide enough to have a stone walkway down the middle. Rectangle-shaped battlements line the outer edge facing the wharf.

When you peek through the battlements, you can see the shadow of a small boat heading toward the wharf. It is time for you to escape.

You have been carrying the rope under your shirt. Now you tie it around a battlement. Then you toss the other end over the edge of the wall. It's time to climb.

But when you reach the end of the rope, you are still dangling in the air. It's dark and you can't tell how far you are from the ground. But down is the only way you can go. Even if you had the strength to pull yourself back up, you would be climbing back to prison and torture.

Turn the page.

You let go. You drop for what seems like forever. Sharp pain shoots up your leg when you hit the ground. But it must not have been a far drop. Other than shock and some immediate pain, you're OK.

"Hurry, guards are coming," you hear someone whisper.

You hobble over to the boat as fast as you can. Your friends tell you to lie down. They cover you with a heavy tarp.

The boat slips away in the night. You are on your way to freedom.

THE END

To follow another path, turn to page 9.
To learn more about the Tower of London, turn to page 101.

You decide a weapon will serve you best. Your friends must have understood your note, because one day you find a dagger tucked into some clothing they have sent.

After a few more secret notes, you arrange for your friends to meet you at the Tower Wharf. Now it's up to you to get there.

On the night of your planned escape, you wait for your guard to bring you dinner. With dagger in hand, you force him to give you his keys. Then you lock him in your cell.

"Stay quiet," you whisper. "I'll see to it you're rewarded for it." He scowls, but nods.

You head down several flights of stairs and exit the tower. Unfortunately the door to the tower is on the inside of the castle. The Tower Wharf, where your friends will meet you, is outside.

Turn the page.

You need to find a door on the outer wall. You look at your guard's keys, but you can't tell which key is for what door.

But you've made a mistake. You have stood in the open for too long. A guard has spotted you.

a view of the River Thames, looking toward the White Tower and the Tower Wharf

"You there, stop!" he shouts.

You try running away from him. But before you get too far, you are met by another guard. With dagger in hand, you attack. He meets your charge with his pike, a long wooden shaft tipped with a steel blade. Trained to watch over the royal prison, the guard is an expert with his weapon. Its long shaft ensures the guard never comes close enough for you to attack. Even if you could get to him, you are only fair at hand-to-hand combat. It's no match. The guard buries the pike's steel tip in your gut. You fall to the ground, the dagger sliding out of your grasp. Death is your escape from the Tower of London.

THE END

To follow another path, turn to page 9.
To learn more about the Tower of London, turn to page 101.

Chapter 4

HELPING A FRIEND ESCAPE

It is a scary time in England. People you once thought of as friends have turned on one another. One remark made at the wrong time can be dangerous—or even deadly.

You are about to see the consequences of trusting the untrustworthy today. In your pocket you carry a note from a good friend. It reads:

I have been accused of a crime and imprisoned in the Tower of London. Please visit, if you can.

You are worried about your friend, so you decide to go. You know that the Tower has a bad reputation. Prisoners there have been brutally tortured, and worse. Some are even publicly executed for their crimes.

Turn the page.

Luckily your friend has not committed any religious crimes. Usually it is heretics who receive the worst treatment. They are often tortured.

Traitors and thieves are treated less harshly. If they are wealthy, they may even hold parties while imprisoned.

Your friend isn't lucky enough to be a noble. But, like most prisoners, your friend is free to have visitors.

If you are visiting your friend William, go to page 73.
If you are visiting your friend Alice, turn to page 78.

When a queen or king dies without an heir, sometimes Parliament chooses the next monarch. That is how George Louis became King George I after the death of his cousin, Queen Anne.

But some thought James Francis Edward Stuart had a better claim to the throne. After all, he was Queen Anne's younger brother.

Your friend William was among those who supported James. He had joined a failed rebellion against the king. For that, William was charged with treason and taken to the Tower of London.

You cross the moat surrounding the castle. You enter the outer wall through the Byward Tower Gate. Then you walk along a stone pathway until you reach the Bloody Tower Gate, which is an entryway into the castle's inner wall.

Turn the page.

William is being held in the Bloody Tower. Once known as the Garden Tower, this building has earned a dark reputation. You climb several flights of stairs to get to your friend's cell.

"How are you, Will?" you ask upon entering his room.

He is sitting at a desk and reading a book. He looks tired, with dark circles under his eyes. You wonder how much weight he has lost in just the short time he has been here.

"OK," he says with a weak smile. Then he looks down at his feet.

"What's wrong?" you ask. "They aren't torturing you, are they?"

"No, no, not for my crimes," he says. "It's just that . . ." He looks up to meet your eyes. "For supporting the rebellion, I'm to be executed."

"When?" you ask, shocked.

"In a matter of days," William replies.

You can't believe what you are hearing.

"I will get you out of here," you whisper to your friend. You have no idea how you will do it. But you promise yourself—and him—that you will.

As your visit continues, he begins to sound more and more hopeful. You think of the way he looked when you first arrived. You think of how heartbroken his family would be if he was gone. There is no way you can fail him. But how will you free him?

On your way out of the castle, you carefully observe the people around you. You hope they might give you some inspiration.

Turn the page.

You notice the yeomen warders in their bright red uniforms. King Henry VII formed this order of the guard at the Tower after he won the War of the Roses in 1485. They are posted at each gate. Others patrol the hallways. They seem to freely go about their business.

Yeoman warders are part of the royal guard. They are also known as beefeaters.

There are also many people wandering around. You guess that some of them live on the castle grounds. But others, like you, must be here to see friends and family who have been imprisoned.

You watch as one couple walks through a tower gate. A yeomen stops the man and checks the package that he carries. The guard does not even question the woman.

An idea is forming. You can have your friend disguise himself. He could put on a yeomen's uniform and simply walk right out of the castle. Or he could dress up as a woman, and you could escort him out.

To disguise your friend as a yeoman, turn to page 81.
To disguise your friend as a woman, turn to page 85.

You are shocked to learn that your friend Alice was jailed for piracy. Usually pirates are sent to regular prison, not the Tower of London. She is also being kept in the Coldharbour Gate, a fort within the inner walls of the castle.

To get to Alice, you had to cross a moat. Then you passed through the outer Byward Tower Gate. After that, you went through the Bloody Tower Gate and into the heart of the fortress.

You stare up at the building. Two cylinder-shaped towers join together to make Coldharbour. They share an edge with the White Tower. Paths edged with battlement walls join the cylinders to the Bloody Tower. This is one of the best-protected places in the entire Tower of London.

"I didn't do it!" Alice says the moment you step into her cell.

You sigh. "Then what *did* happen?" you ask.

"It was the captain of the ship I was aboard," she says. "He stole a chest of gold that belonged to the king and laid the blame on me."

Alice is your friend. She is not a thief, and she definitely is not foolish enough to steal from the king. That is a crime that could lead to harsh punishment.

"Did they say how long you are to be held here?" you ask.

"Until the king gets his gold back," she answers, frowning. "At least, that is what I've been told."

It could be a long time until they find the treasure—if they ever find it. You feel that your friend has been falsely accused of a crime. You want to get her out of here. That means helping her escape, if you can.

Turn the page.

"I will find a way to get you out," you say gallantly.

"But how?" she asks.

You peek out the cell's tiny window. It would be easy enough for her to squeeze out. All she would need is a rope. She could use it to lower herself down to the ground.

You examine the rest of the cell. You notice something odd about the door. There is a wide gap underneath, and the bolt holding the single hinge is loose. Someone could pry it open with the right tool.

What do you smuggle into the Tower to help Alice escape?

To smuggle in a rope, turn to page 87.
To smuggle in a stick, turn to page 90.

If you dress William as a guard, he'll also be armed. The thought of a backup weapon gives you a sense of confidence and security.

First, you need a yeoman's uniform. You bribe a local tailor to make one for you. He makes some of the clothes for the nobles in the Tower and knows what the uniforms look like in detail. You pay well, and he works fast.

Next, you need to sneak the uniform into William's cell. For that, you ask for help from another friend, Betty. Each of you hides part of the disguise under your normal clothes. Betty also carries the boots in a bag she covers with a blanket.

All goes well when you enter the castle. Guards nod to you as you walk through the gates. No one checks the bag that Betty carries.

Turn the page.

You head up the flights of stairs to William's room. He quickly changes while Betty stands guard.

Everything is set. Now you just need to make it out of the castle.

You and Betty will leave first. Then William will follow. If all goes as planned, you will meet on the other side of the moat.

You walk down the stairway and then linger at the bottom. William is not far behind. People step aside for him out of respect.

You hold your breath as you walk through the Bloody Tower, but nobody stops you. Now just through the Byward Tower Gate, and William will be free.

But about halfway to the outer gate, someone calls out. "You there. What are you doing here?"

The Bloody Tower entrance allows visitors to pass through the inner wall.

You glance behind to see a couple of the guards blocking William's path.

"I don't recognize you," one guard says.

"I'm new," William tries to explain.

Turn the page.

The first guard shakes his head. Then he takes a closer look at William's face. "You look like that prisoner up in the Bloody Tower."

William panics. As the guards begin to grapple with him, you and Betty turn and walk calmly away. You cannot help him. You cannot afford to be captured. You have no other choice.

That night, you receive news from William. His execution has been moved to the next day. Time is up. You have lost your opportunity to save your friend.

THE END

To follow another path, turn to page 9.
To learn more about the Tower of London, turn to page 101

The yeomen all live at the castle. You are afraid that they will notice a new face in uniform. They might even recognize him as a prisoner. The way the guards ignored the women at the fortress makes you confident that disguising William as a woman is the best choice.

For William's disguise, you get help from another friend, Betty. She agrees to wear two dresses and carry a wig and makeup with her into the castle.

The next day, you both go to see William. You pass by guards at each gate. Not one of them checks the bag that Betty carries. They are used to seeing you come and go.

Inside his cell, William changes into the spare dress. You and Betty help him with the wig and makeup.

Turn the page.

You take a step back. While it is not a perfect disguise, it will do—as long as no one stops William and looks too closely.

"Now what?" he asks.

The guards saw you and Betty enter the tower together. Although you don't feel as though they paid you a lot of attention, they might have. They will be expecting two people to walk out together. Three people leaving together at the same time would be too obvious.

You could send William out first, by himself. Then you and Betty could follow. But would it be safer for Betty and William to leave as a pair?

To send William and Betty together, turn to page 92.
To make William go alone, turn to page 94.

If you bring Alice a rope, she can escape on her own. You hide the rope in a package of clothing. It is actually not uncommon for people to bring things to people staying in the prison. You have no doubts that this idea will work.

But as you pass through one of the castle's gates, a yeoman stops you.

"What do you have there?" he asks.

"Just some clothes for a friend," you say.

"Let's have a look then," he says.

"Are you sure?" you ask. You fumble, trying to find a coin to slip him.

"Are you trying to bribe me?" the guard roars. His face turns as red as his uniform. "I'm one of the king's royal bodyguard, and you think I can be bribed? With that?"

Turn the page.

Other guards have appeared. They hold you and search your things. They find the rope right away. Then you are taken to the White Tower.

"You think it's easy to escape the Tower?" the guard asks. "Let's see you get out of Little Ease."

Little Ease is in part of the dungeon under the White Tower. It is only 4 feet (1.2 meters) square and has no windows.

"No," you beg. "Not there!" You have heard the stories. Little Ease is the most famous torture cell. It is only a few feet wide and a few feet tall. It is not tall enough for you to stand in, and it's not long enough for you to lie down.

When you see the heavy wooden door, you struggle to get free. But there is no escape. The guard shoves you inside and the door slams shut behind you.

You are in darkness for what could be eternity. The time spent in Little Ease is horrible. You are cold and sore from lying curled up in a ball on the stone floor. You have no idea when you will get out—if ever.

THE END

To follow another path, turn to page 9.
To learn more about the Tower of London, turn to page 101.

It would be easy enough for Alice to squeeze out of a window and crawl out of her cell. But then what? Someone would likely see her scaling down the side of a tower. Instead, you will bring her a stick. You hope she can use it to pry open her cell door.

When a yeoman sees it tucked in with the other things you are bringing Alice, he gives you an odd look.

"She likes to whittle," you lie.

The guard shrugs but lets you by. What he does not notice is that the clothes you carry are actually from your own closet.

The plan is for Alice to work on the loose hinge with the stick. She should be able to get the door open enough to slip out unnoticed. Then she will leave, dressed in some of your clothes.

The guards have seen you visiting her often. You are both small and slim, and your hair is a similar length and color. You hope that they will assume she is you.

You also make a point to say hello to the guards every time you visit. You want them to be used to seeing you coming and going. You also always wear the same outfit, which is similar to the clothes you brought Alice.

On the day of her escape, you need to decide where you'll be. Will you wait outside the castle for Alice and let her sneak out herself? Or should you visit one last time to help with her escape?

To wait, turn to page 96.
To go see her, turn to page 98.

"You two go ahead," you say. "I will stay."

You watch as your friends leave. They walk arm in arm down the hallway. When a guard approaches, William looks down and whispers something in Betty's ear. The guard walks past without blinking.

Meanwhile, in William's cell, you pretend to have a conversation with William.

"It looks like nice weather we are having," you say, trying to sound like your friend.

"Yes, it is a lovely day," you say in your voice.

"Do you have any news of my family?" your "friend" asks.

You continue on like this with hope that the guards will not get suspicious. You want them to think that William is still in his cell.

When you tire of talking to yourself, you leave the cell. By now, your friends should be well clear of the main gate. You quietly slip out and close the door behind you.

"I wouldn't bother the prisoner," you say to the guard on duty. "He's sleeping."

The guard simply nods as he walks by.

You see Will again at your house. While he has escaped the Tower of London, you know that he is far from safe. He will have to flee England. But living far from home will be better than having to face the executioner.

THE END

To follow another path, turn to page 9.
To learn more about the Tower of London, turn to page 101.

The guards saw you and Betty enter the Bloody Tower together. It might be odd if you do not leave together too.

So you have William leave first. You and Betty count to 100 and then follow.

As you approach the exit to the tower, you can see a small crowd forming. You are horrified to see that the yeoman guarding the tower has grabbed William.

"Well, what have we here?" the guard asks, smirking and poking William.

William says nothing.

"I don't recall you entering the tower," another yeoman says.

"Looks kind of like one of our prisoners," the first says. "Only in a bad disguise." He grabs the wig from William's head. The crowd cheers.

You and Betty try to hurry through the gate before anyone notices. But you're not fast enough. A yeoman spots you.

"You there!" he shouts. "You were visiting this prisoner!"

You do not know what else to do but to turn and run. Betty follows. But the crowd has grown too large and there is nowhere to go. You are quicky cornered and caught.

You and Betty are thrown into a cell. You are not allowed to leave until after William's execution.

THE END

To follow another path, turn to page 9.
To learn more about the Tower of London, turn to page 101.

You decide to meet Alice at your house. You worry that if you go to the prison today, the guards might notice two people dressed alike.

Instead, you prepare for Alice to leave the country once she escapes. The authorities will be looking for her. It won't be safe for her to stay in the area. You pack some of her things and arrange passage aboard a ship headed to France.

Then you wait.

And wait.

The sun sinks below the horizon, and there is still no sign of your friend. You begin to worry.

But then you hear a soft rap on your door. You peek outside, and there she is.

"Quick, get inside," you say.

The conflict between Roman Catholics and Protestants was known as the English Civil War (1642–1651).

"Sorry it took me so long," she says. "I wanted to make sure nobody tried to stop and talk to me. I had to take a roundabout way to get here."

None of that matters now. Alice is safe!

THE END

To follow another path, turn to page 9.
To learn more about the Tower of London, turn to page 101.

You decide to go to the prison one last time. You want to make sure Alice has everything she needs to escape. And you can't just sit at home waiting and wondering.

Like every other visit, you nod to the yeomen guarding Coldharbour. This time, though, he stops you. "Weren't you here earlier?" he asks.

"N-no," you stammer.

"Are you sure?" he asks, squinting. "I swear I saw someone . . ." He frowns. "I better take you up."

Nervous, you follow him up the stairs. You don't like this. He knows you know where to go. You don't need a guide.

When you reach the cell, you can see that the door has been pried open. You arrived too late. Alice has already escaped.

The guard turns to you. "You helped her, didn't you? I knew I saw someone dressed like this before."

You yell and scream, but they ignore you. You are shoved into the cell that was once Alice's.

"We are keeping you here until we find her," a guard says. "Then we'll decide what to do."

Another guard secures the door. He breaks the stick in two before tossing it out the window. Then he tightens the door's loose hinges.

If the guards find Alice, she will surely be punished. If they do not catch her, you have no idea when you will be let out of the cell.

All you can do is wait and hope your punishment is not too severe.

THE END

To follow another path, turn to page 9.
To learn more about the Tower of London, turn to page 101.

Chapter 5

THE TOWER OF LONDON

In 1066 William the Conqueror defeated several powerful English lords at the Battle of Hastings. With this victory, he sealed his claim to the English throne. William then went on to unite all of England under his rule. He served as king of England until his death in 1087.

William had the Tower built on the outskirts of London, near the banks of the River Thames. The Tower provided a place for William to rule from. It also protected the city from attack.

As new rulers came into power, the castle grew. A ring of smaller towers was built around the White Tower. These smaller towers were connected by walls to encircle the castle grounds. An outer wall was eventually added.

A moat was dug and filled with water from the River Thames. Other buildings were constructed, such as a chapel and a barracks for soldiers. Over time, the single tower that William had built became a fortress. Today, all of its buildings and towers are collectively known as the Tower of London.

Among the Tower's many uses, it is best known for being a prison and a place of cruel torture. Its history of famous inmates and executions has also earned the Tower of London the reputation of being one of the most haunted places in the world. Many people believe that the spirits of people who were killed there roam the grounds. There are even stories of a ghostly bear, believed to have once been part of the Royal Menagerie.

Over the course of its history, thousands of people have been imprisoned in the castle. Prisoners range from traitors to the crown to spies, assassins, corrupt government officials, religious heretics, and deposed kings and queens. Most were eventually released. Hundreds were executed for their crimes. And nearly 40 people actually escaped.

The first to do so was Ranulf Flambard in 1100. He simply held a party for some of the guards and then snuck out while they were distracted. Others used disguises. Some escapees had ropes smuggled in and climbed down the castle's walls. Prisoners have swum across the moat or had boats pick them up at the Tower Wharf. One inmate actually used orange juice as invisible ink to send secret messages to friends to arrange an escape.

The Tower of London did not have the security measures that modern prisons have. As a result, many escape stories sound surprisingly simple and even somewhat unbelievable. But when they were taking place, prisoners were treated very differently. Most were allowed to roam the castle grounds with only a guard watching over them. Some even bribed their guards to let them wander around by themselves.

The White Tower has four stories. The entrance is on the first story, not the ground floor.

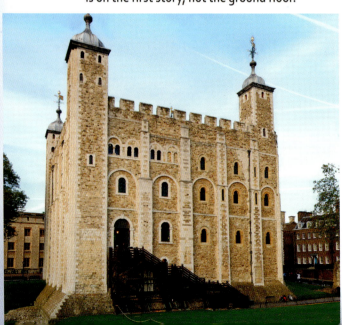

Wealthy people could have food and clothes brought in to them. This gave them a chance to have items like ropes and weapons smuggled in with other supplies.

Today, the Tower of London serves other purposes. It is no longer used as the country's seat of power or as a prison. Now it is mostly a museum and a tourist attraction. Stories of the ghosts lurking about its grounds and the many strange escape attempts attract visitors from all over the world. Some also come to see the Crown Jewels, which are locked away in the Jewel House. It is an incredible place to visit and study.

TIMELINE

CHAPTER 2: A TRAITOR AND SPY

June 1377: Edward III dies

1377: Richard II rules

1399: Henry IV rules

1413: Henry V rules

1422: Henry VI rules

1455: The War of the Roses starts when Richard, Duke of York, leads the Yorks at the First Battle of St. Albans

1461: Edward IV rules; he is the first York king

1470: Henry VI takes the crown back

1471: Edward IV takes the crown back

1483: Edward V rules from April 9 to June 25

1483: Richard III rules; he is the last York king

1485: Henry Tudor defeats Richard III at the Battle of Bosworth Field; this ends the War of the Roses; Henry marries Edward IV's daughter, Elizabeth, and crowns himself Henry VII

CHAPTER 3: RELIGIOUS PERSECUTION

1547: Edward VI rules

1553: Mary I rules

1558: Mary I dies; Elizabeth I is crowned

CHAPTER 4: HELPING A FRIEND ESCAPE

1714: George Louis is crowned; he rules until 1727

REAL ESCAPE ATTEMPTS

1100: Ranulf Flambard became the Tower of London's first official prisoner. He was also its first escapee. Flambard was jailed for being a corrupt government official. Because he was wealthy, he could afford to have food and wine brought to him while imprisoned. In a barrel of oysters, he had a rope smuggled into the Tower. One night, he invited the guards into his cell for a celebration. While the guards were busy, Flambard slipped away. He squeezed through a window and used the rope to lower himself to the ground.

1413: Sir John Oldcastle was labeled a heretic by his enemies. His religious views differed from those of the Catholic Church. This led to his imprisonment in the Tower of London.

But Oldcastle was popular amongst his supporters. They liked that he voiced his opinions and stood up for those who shared his beliefs. Instead of sneaking him out, his friends snuck into the castle and broke him out. Time and time again, Oldcastle narrowly escaped recapture. But his luck ran out in 1417, when he was finally caught and sent back to the Tower. Shortly afterward, he was hanged over a burning pyre.

1597: John Gerard was a Catholic priest who was persecuted after Protestants came into power. He was captured in 1594 and sent to the Tower in April 1587. Kept in the Salt Tower, he was repeatedly tortured, but never gave up any information.

With the warder's help, Gerard was able to obtain writing materials to send messages to his friends. But he did not just ask for pen and ink. He also asked for a sack of oranges. Using orange juice, he was able to hide secret messages on the letters. The messages, written in juice, could only be seen if the paper was heated. Gerard was able to arrange for a prison break through these secret messages.

One night in 1597, he and another prisoner, John Arden, made their escape. Arden had been kept in the Salt Tower, which was next to the Cradle Tower. The men became friends. They convinced guards to let them meet to pray.

Gerard asked his friends to bring a rope to the Tower. One end of the rope would be staked across the moat. They brought the other end of the rope to the wall. Gerard let down a length of heavy thread, which his friends tied to the rope. Gerard was then able to pull the rope to the top of the tower.

Gerard and Arden slid down the rope and across the moat and to the wharf. There, Gerard's friends were waiting with a boat as a getaway vehicle.

Gerard took care to protect his warder from punishment. He arranged for the warder's passage to a safe house and gave him money to replace his lost wages.

Although free, Gerard eventually had to leave the country. He slipped out disguised as a servant to the Spanish ambassador.

1716: The Earl of Nithsdale was sent to the Tower of London for treason. He had supported one of the king's rivals. Days before he was to be executed, his wife and her maid came to visit. Under their clothes, they snuck in a disguise for the earl. He dressed up as a woman. His wife even brought him a wig and white makeup to cover up his beard.

The Earl and the maid walked out of the castle. His wife stayed behind in his cell. She pretended to talk to her husband so that the guards would not get suspicious about the escape attempt. They did not realize that the earl had left his cell until he was safely away.

OTHER PATHS TO EXPLORE

◈ Prisoners at the Tower of London had a surprising amount of freedom. Some were able to bribe their warders into letting them visit other inmates. How might being able to talk to another prisoner aid in your escape plans?

◈ The Tower of London is thought to be one of the most haunted places in the world. Many people have died there cruelly, from Queen Anne Boleyn, the second wife to King Henry VIII, to Lady Jane Grey. She was queen for just nine days before Mary I took the crown from her and had her executed. The ghosts of both Anne Boleyn and Jane Grey are said to haunt the castle. How might one of the many ghosts lurking about the Tower of London help in planning an escape?

◈ One means of planning an escape was by sending secret messages to friends. One escapee actually used orange juice like an invisible ink to send such messages. But there are many other ways, from messenger pigeons to secrets codes that can be used to send messages. What other methods could be used to send messages as well as get items into (or out of) the castle?

READ MORE

Boutland, Craig. *Ghoulish Ghosts*. Minneapolis: Lerner Publications, 2019.

Hoena, Blake. *Tower of London: A Chilling Interactive Adventure*. North Mankato, MN: Capstone Press, 2017.

Pascal, Janet B. *Where is the Tower of London?* New York: Penguin Workshop, an imprint of Penguin Random House, 2018.

INTERNET SITES

Historic Royal Palaces: Tower of London
http://www.hrp.org.uk/TowerOfLondon

History Channel: 6 Famous Prisoners of the Tower of London
https://www.history.com/news/6-famous-prisoners-of-the-tower-of-london

UNESCO: Tower of London
https://whc.unesco.org/en/list/488

INDEX

COULD YOU ESCAPE ALCATRAZ?

BY ERIC BRAUN

CAPSTONE PRESS

a capstone imprint

You Choose Books are published by Capstone Press
1710 Roe Crest Drive, North Mankato, Minnesota 56003
www.capstonepub.com

Library of Congress Cataloging-in-Publication Data
Names: Braun, Eric, 1971– author.
Title: Could you escape Alcatraz? : an interactive survival adventure / by
  Eric Braun.
Description: North Mankato, Minnesota : Capstone Press, [2020] | Series: You
  choose: can you escape? | Summary: Cast as a prisoner in the infamous
  Alcatraz Penitentiary, the reader's choices determine if escape is
  possible.
Identifiers: LCCN 2019006018| ISBN 9781543573923 (hardcover) | ISBN
  9781543575613 (paperback) | ISBN 9781543573961 (ebook pdf)
Subjects: LCSH: Plot-your-own stories. | CYAC: Prisoners—Fiction. |
  Escapes—Fiction. | United States Penitentiary, Alcatraz Island,
  California—Fiction. | Plot-your-own stories.
Classification: LCC PZ7.1.B751542 Cou 2019 | DDC [Fic]—dc23
LC record available at https://lccn.loc.gov/2019006018

Editorial Credits
Mari Bolte, editor; Bobbie Nuytten, designer; Eric Gohl, media researcher:
Laura Manthe, premedia specialist

Photo Credits
AP Photo: Clarence Hamm, 72, Ernest K. Bennett, 99; Eric Gohl: 37, 42, 94, 105;
Getty Images: Anadolu Agency, 24, Bettmann, 21, 91; Library of Congress: 66, 77,
87; Newscom: Everett Collection, 4, 6; Shutterstock: Arne Beruldsen, 63, brian takes
photos, 51, Clari Massimiliano, 29, kenkistler, 83, Milan Sommer, 47, MintImages, 34,
Nick Heinimann, 10, PeanutsNSoda, cover, back cover, superjoseph, 102; Wikimedia:
NPS, 17, 56

Printed and bound in China. PO4940

TABLE OF CONTENTS

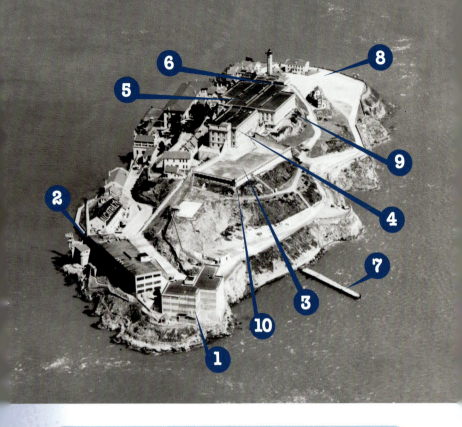

Map Key:

1. maintenance shop
2. power house
3. prison yard
4. hall and kitchen
5. main cell block
6. administration and warden's office
7. dock
8. guard recreation yard
9. catwalk
10. guard tower

ABOUT YOUR ADVENTURE

YOU are about to become a prisoner at the infamous Alcatraz Federal Penitentiary. Nicknamed "The Rock", it is famous for keeping dangerous prisoners from escaping. But that won't stop you from trying.

Start the story. Then follow the directions at the bottom of each page. You may have done wrong in the past, but the choices you make will change the outcome. After you finish one path, go back and read the others to see how the decisions you make change your fate. Do you have what it takes to make it off The Rock?

Turn the page to begin your adventure.

Chapter 1

A HARD LIFE ON THE ROCK

You're here—the famous Alcatraz Island. The prison sits 1.25 miles (2.4 kilometers) away from the mainland of San Francisco. That's a long swim to freedom.

To get here, you were delivered by boat across cold, choppy water. You and other prisoners were shackled and watched closely by armed guards. When the boat docked, you looked up at the prison—high walls made of stone and brick, and topped with barbed wire. Frigid wind tussled your hair and chilled your skin.

As you stepped onto the island, you were searched and given a prison uniform. Then you were assigned to a cell.

Turn the page.

All this time, you looked carefully around you, noting every detail of your surroundings. How high the fence was, how long the hallway, how thick the iron bars. Already thinking of escape. Could it be done?

Everyone says Alcatraz is inescapable. Now that you've been here a while, you have to admit, it just might be. Even if you were to somehow get out of your cell, out of the building, over the walls, past the machine gun towers, and across the bay to the mainland, then what? You would be cold, wet, without money or transportation . . . and you'd be wearing a prison uniform. Blending in would be a real problem. Where would you go after that?

But here's an even bigger problem: Life on The Rock is hard. It's boring, harsh, and often violent. Meanwhile, a life of freedom teases you like the sunshine that occasionally peeks over the high prison yard walls.

Maybe no one has escaped The Rock before. Maybe you won't be able to either. But you have to give it a shot. Success will depend on the person you choose to be. Pick wisely!

To be an athlete with great strength and endurance, turn to page 11.

To be a highly intelligent criminal mastermind, turn to page 43.

To be a mechanic who can build anything, turn to page 73.

Chapter 2

THE ATHLETE PLAYS FOR KEEPS

You were a star athlete in high school. In football, you were a running back, fast and bruising. In baseball, you played first base and hit home runs. Maybe most important of all, you were a record-setting swimmer. You were happy.

But then your father died. You had no choice but to drop out of school to take a job. You had to help pay rent and buy food for you, your little brother, and mom. You worked your fingers to the bone at an auto plant.

Even with your job, money was tight. To make ends meet, you started to steal from stores. Soon you graduated to robbing people, then to robbing banks. You got away with it for a while.

Turn the page.

But then your luck ran out. Eventually you were caught and sent to prison. When you got out, you went right back to robbing. What else could you do? Your family was desperate.

The second time you went to prison, you overpowered a guard while working in a field. You hid in the woods for three days before being caught. The judge sent you to The Rock so you couldn't escape again.

Now you lie on your cot at night and remember your days as a sports star. You miss those old, simpler times.

You also worry about your family. You would love to see your mom and brother again. And so you plan your escape. The way you see it, there are two ways to do it.

To rely on your strength and speed, go to page 13.
To take a more sneaky approach, turn to page 15.

Your athletic abilities are your greatest tools. You might as well use them.

You're not thrilled with the idea of using violence, but you're sure it's your best chance. If you don't escape, you will be killed in a fight or sent to solitary—a small, pitch-black cell all by yourself. Solitary can drive a person insane. Just the threat is enough to keep most men from trying to escape.

You will need help to pull this off. After dinner one night, a guard passes your cell, making his rounds. When he's out of earshot, you step up to the front corner of your cell and whisper to the man in the next cell over. Hanson is not strong like you, but he's been on The Rock a long time. He knows its secrets. He's also your friend. You trust him.

Turn the page.

"Hanson," you whisper. "Let's see the moon."

This is code for getting out. Nobody in Alcatraz ever sees the moon because they're locked up at night.

Hanson is silent a moment. Perhaps he is stunned by your proposal. Then comes his barely audible reply: "Yes."

Over the next few nights, you talk at the front of your cells, making a plan. Hanson has a job in the maintenance shop in the Model Industries building and says only two guards are on duty on weekends.

To try to get a job in maintenance with Hanson, turn to page 16.

To have Hanson steal a weapon from the shop, turn to page 18.

Fighting and running can only end in disaster. You'll have better luck if you can find a way to sneak out.

Not long after you make this decision, you are assigned a job in the kitchen. Every day you help unload groceries that are delivered on a boat. Wooden crates of meat. Sacks of flour and rice. Big plastic racks of milk jugs. Boxes of canned goods. It's not the most interesting job in the world, but it's a change of pace.

Twice a week, bags of bread arrive at the kitchen inside a huge wooden crate. As you unload bread from the box one day, you realize that it is just big enough to fit a person inside if you sit with your knees tight to your chest. These bread crates could be the key to your escape.

To try to escape inside a bread box, turn to page 20.
To wait for another, more complete plan, turn to page 23.

Within a couple weeks, Hanson is able to get you a job in the maintenance shop. You work side-by-side with a couple other prisoners. Just like Hanson said, two guards work on weekends. As long as you stay focused on your job and don't cause any trouble, the guards leave you alone.

The only windows in the maintenance shop are reinforced with heavy steel bars. But if you can get through the bars, you'll be outside the prison walls and right next to the sea. The Model Industries building is at the northernmost point of the island. It might be a while before you're missed.

Hanson tells you of an old rumor: a convict once stole a life jacket and hid it in the bushes down the beach from the maintenance shop. He is confident that it's still there. If you make it to the water, you can take turns resting on the life jacket and float to safety.

Tool-proof steel bars replaced the plain metal bars over the windows in 1934.

Should you let the other two prisoners in on the plot? Can you trust them? Maybe they can help. Ramstad is a big man, and he could help in many ways. Kelly is a cold-blooded murderer. A guy like that could be useful—or turn on you.

No matter what, you *have* to tell them something. They will be in the room when you attack the guards. You need them ready.

To invite Ramstad and Kelly to join you, turn to page 26.

To ask for their help, turn to page 27.

Hanson can't get metal through the metal detector at the shop, so he steals a block of wood. At dinner one night, he talks to his friend Stinky about a saw blade that he hid long ago when he worked in the laundry room. Stinky is on the side of anyone who might escape. He agrees to retrieve the blade.

It arrives hidden in a bundle of clean sheets at Hanson's cell. That night after lights-out, Hanson wraps one end of the blade in a towel to make a handle and saws the hunk of wood into a dagger.

Later, he sneaks another block of wood and the saw blade to you. Now it's your turn to fashion a dagger. You have a close call that night when you drop the metal saw. It clangs on the concrete floor. You quickly hide the blade and wooden dagger behind some books on your shelf and get in bed.

The guard comes to your cell and shines his light inside. You squint up at him and act as if he just woke you. You try to look sleepy, but inside your heart is racing.

Thankfully, the guard casts his light around your cell and walks past.

Will he tell the other guards about the metallic sound? Will they be watching you?

To plan your escape for as soon as possible, turn to page 29.

To wait until the heat dies down, turn to page 31.

You enlist two trusted friends in the kitchen to help you. Late one afternoon, an inmate named Stinky starts a fight with another inmate in the kitchen. This is all part of the plan. When the guards go to break it up, you quickly climb into the box, and your friend clasps it shut.

You feel yourself being lifted gracefully, and then you are on the move. Before long you smell the salty ocean air, and your heart fills with excitement. You're outside!

Then you hear a voice calling. It's Lieutenant French, one of the guards.

"Hold it!" he says. "Why does that empty box look so heavy? Open it up."

You feel the box clunk on the dock. Outside, your friend Ginger Mac says, "It ain't heavy, what're you talking about?"

Footsteps approach the box. You do not allow yourself a breath.

"You want me to open it up?" Ginger Mac says. "It's empty." He starts to undo one of the clasps.

But French says, "Just load it up."

You feel yourself lifted once again. Next time you come down, you know you are inside the cargo bay of a boat. Soon, the boat leaves the dock.

Turn the page.

A guard tower overlooks the pier where visitors tie up their boats.

Once your shift in the kitchen is over, they will do a count and realize you're missing. You don't have much time. So you kick open the box and creep to the front of the cargo bay. Sea air whips all around you.

You dive over the railing and plunge into the cold water.

It's dark outside by the time the patrol boats are out. They sweep their searchlights across the surface. You swim underwater as much as you can. You make it to land and crawl up a rocky beach, panting and cold. You hide in a cliff opening.

The next morning you hear helicopters in the air. And you hear dogs patrolling the beach. You realize it's only a matter of time before you're caught.

THE END

To follow another path, turn to page 9.
To learn more about Alcatraz, turn to page 103.

Sneaking out of prison in a bread box? It's just too ridiculous. It would never work.

Instead, you spend the next few weeks playing chess with some of the other inmates in the yard during outdoor time. You manage to make friends with Papa, a powerful gangster. One day, over a game of chess, you tell Papa about your desire to escape. You ask for his advice.

He looks up at the squawking seagulls for a few seconds. Then he says, very quietly, "Let me talk to someone."

Four days later, you are playing chess with Papa again. He takes your rook with his queen. "Check," he says. Then, quieter, he says, "Get real sick. Sickest you've ever been. There's a bar spreader taped under the second bed in the infirmary."

Turn the page.

A day later you're in your cell eating an old, dead rat that you found and stashed. Its body is crawling with insects and decay.

At dinner that night you become violently ill and are carried to the infirmary. Someone takes your vital signs and hooks you up to an IV. You keep retching. You hope you're not actually too sick to make your escape.

According to Alcatraz regulations, prisoners were entitled to food, clothing, shelter, and medical attention.

Later, loud noises echo from the hallway. You remember that Papa promised a distraction. The guard leaves to check it out. You pull out the IV and reach for the bar spreader—basically a long rod. You use it to knock out the nurse.

You lock the door, climb on top of the bed, and open the window. You pry the bars behind the window apart.

You dash into the ocean. It's freezing. *You're strong*, you remind yourself. But as you push your body to its limits, you throw up. Your head starts to spin.

You realize you are too weak to make this trip. You will drown if you continue. You have to swim back and turn yourself in.

THE END

To follow another path, turn to page 9.
To learn more about Alcatraz, turn to page 103.

Those two prisoners are not going to solitary to help you, that's for sure. The smart thing to do would be to invite them along. Hanson runs a grinder to cover his voice while he tells them your plan. Ramstad and Kelly tell Hanson they want to talk about it. They'll let you know tomorrow.

Something about the exchange doesn't sit right with you. Why would they have to talk it over? They might be planning to turn you in.

That night you and Hanson gather at the corners of your adjoining cells. You whisper, "I don't like it."

"They're solid," Hanson says back. He means you can trust them.

"It doesn't feel right," you say.

If you trust Kelly and Ramstad, turn to page 33.
If you decide to make a new plan, turn to page 36.

Most men on The Rock would love to see it "broken"—to see someone escape. You figure that includes Kelly and Ramstad. So Hanson lets them in on your plan. He asks them to keep the guards tied up while you get as far as you can.

"So we just stay here while you get away?" Ramstad says. He runs the drill press as he speaks, and the noise covers your conversation.

"This puts us in a bad spot," Kelly adds.

"I'm up for parole next year," Ramstad says, frowning. If he helps you, he'll never get parole.

You'll have to think of another way. But the next day, your cell is "tossed." The warden and two guards come and search it thoroughly. They turn over your mattress. They check between the pages of your books. They look under your sink. They even squirt out your toothpaste.

Turn the page.

They find nothing. They question you, but you tell them nothing.

You know that Ramstad ratted you out. Helping the guys in charge will show that he's a changed man. This will strengthen his case for parole. You wish there was a way to get revenge on him before he gets out, but there isn't. You just have to watch him go free and keep waiting for your own chance.

THE END

To follow another path, turn to page 9.
To learn more about Alcatraz, turn to page 103.

The next day, you and Hanson hide your wooden daggers inside your jackets. He has gotten approval to have you help him in the maintenance shop for the day. You plan to stab your guard on the way there. Then you should be able to get over the fence and into the water before anyone knows you're missing.

Turn the page.

The fences around Alcatraz were 12 feet (3.7 meters) high and topped with barbed wire and razor wire.

The plan seems pretty solid. As a state champion swimmer, you know that you'll be able to make it all the way to shore. As for Hanson, who knows?

Unfortunately, you don't get a chance to try your plan. You were right about heat being on you. When the guards come to your cell, they tell you to leave your jacket and shoes in the cell. Then more guards come—and so does the warden. You know this is not good news.

As you watch, the guards "toss," or search, your cell. They find the saw blade in a book and the dagger in your jacket. Hanson gets searched too. You and Hanson exchange a sad look before the guards lead you to solitary confinement.

THE END

To follow another path, turn to page 9.
To learn more about Alcatraz, turn to page 103.

If the guard tells anyone what he heard, you could be in trouble. Nervous, you call off the escape attempt.

Two days later, you learn that you were right: They *were* onto you. While you are in the mess hall, the warden and two guards come into your cell and search it. They find the weapon and the saw blade. And, knowing that you are friends with Hanson, they also search his cell. They find his dagger as well.

You are sent to solitary. It is dark, lonely, and silent. The cell is tiny. You have to fight every day to keep your wits—it feels like you're going insane. You've always been strong physically. Mental toughness is a different thing. How long have you been here? You've lost track.

Turn the page.

Wait—was that a voice? It can't be. Nobody is here. But in the dark you can't be sure.

It *was* a voice. You're sure of it. Kind of.

It's your mother. Can that be right? It sounds like her. She scolds you for robbing those people. She didn't raise you like that. You knew it was wrong. What were you thinking?

She loves you though. She misses you. It's nice to hear her voice.

THE END

To follow another path, turn to page 9.
To learn more about Alcatraz, turn to page 103.

You hear from Kelly and Ramstad soon enough: They're in.

And the news is even better than you hoped. Ramstad has a girlfriend in San Francisco. She will hide you—if you can get there.

Early in your shift the next day, Kelly strikes one guard across the face with a wrench. Hanson and Ramstad beat the other with their hands while you take a long metal file to the window. The other three tie up the bleeding guards with an electrical cord.

"Hurry, hurry," Kelly mutters at you. You work as fast as you can, your hands getting shredded as you go. When you get through the bar, you use the wrench to pry the bar away from the window.

Turn the page.

Outside, Hanson finds the hidden life jacket. The four of you wade into the water, then swim as fast as you can. You trade off holding onto the life jacket so you each get short rests. Still, the trip is exhausting. At least the waves are mild.

The water around Alcatraz is usually very cold, around 60 degrees Fahrenheit (15.5 degrees Celsius).

You wash up on a beach and walk north for nearly a mile along the jagged coast. You pass a group of seals sunning on some big rocks. You imagine the authorities will be searching for you now.

Finally, you reach a set of stairs. At the top, sitting in a blue pickup truck, is Ramstad's girlfriend. You lay in the truck bed out of sight until you reach her apartment.

Once there, the woman heats up a couple cans of soup. You've made it! At least for now. You try to relax, but every sound makes you jump. For the rest of your life you'll be looking over your shoulder. But for now, you eat your soup and enjoy being free.

THE END

To follow another path, turn to page 9.
To learn more about Alcatraz, turn to page 103.

You don't know Kelly and Ramstad very well. It's not worth the risk. You let them know the escape is off. Now, you wait.

It is months before you get another chance. You put in a transfer out of maintenance and onto the garbage crew. You and Hanson devise a plan to get transported out of the prison with the garbage. When the load is dumped at the loading dock, you tumble out with the garbage. Hanson breaks his arm in the fall. It smells so awful that Hanson throws up on himself. You just tell him to keep the noise down.

After dark, you climb out of the garbage into the water. But you're only a few hundred yards out into the ocean before Hanson starts to struggle. He wasn't a very strong guy to begin with. With the broken arm, he's even weaker.

The water currents around the island are strong and unpredicatable.

"Float on your back," you call to him. You put an arm around his chest and pull him toward you. You sidestroke toward the mainland, dragging Hanson with you. But before long, you start to get tired too.

To let him go, turn to page 38.
To keep helping him, turn to page 40.

You realize you have no choice if you want to live. You can either let him slip into the water and drown, giving yourself a chance to survive, or you hold on—and drown with him.

"I'm sorry!" you yell as you release him. Suddenly he has more energy than he did before. He grasps and claws at you with his good arm. Terror fills his eyes. "I'm sorry!" you say again. It is a terrible moment. But it only takes a few seconds for you to get away. He doesn't say any last words, just disappears in the dark waves.

You turn toward the mainland and swim harder. Your strokes are smooth and efficient. At the beach, you find a small parking lot. It's empty except for one car. Inside, a man and woman are sitting arm in arm.

You grab a large rock off the beach and run toward the driver's door. You pull the door open and pull him out. He's about your size. You lift the rock high.

"Take off your clothes!" you yell.

He does. The sweater is a little tight across your broad chest and you can't button the pants, but it will do. You leave the two of them in the parking lot and drive away in their car.

As you drive, you try to decide where to go. Maybe there's a map in the glove compartment. And you'll need to fill the car's tank eventually. The important thing for now, though, is to just keep going.

THE END

To follow another path, turn to page 9.
To learn more about Alcatraz, turn to page 103.

It might be hopeless, but you just can't leave your friend to drown. So despite feeling tired, you keep on pulling him through the water. Slowly, you make your way across the bay. The sun comes up. You see that you are still several hundred yards from shore.

A sharp cramp develops in your left hamstring. It's so deep and painful, you actually scream. You can't move your leg, and for a second you taste seawater in your mouth. You're slipping. Furiously, you pump your other leg and your free arm and get above water again. You take deep breaths. Hanson is kicking too, but it's not much help. You taste the water again.

Just rest a second, you think.

And you relax. Your two bodies float for a moment, then start going down. You let them. The rest helps. You can feel strength trickle back into your limbs. You kick again, and you rise to the surface. Your teeth are chattering. Your look at your fingers—they're blue.

You sink again.

You pump your legs, but it's not enough. You sink. And sink.

You can't feel anything.

THE END

To follow another path, turn to page 9.
To learn more about Alcatraz, turn to page 103.

Chapter 3

THE MASTERMIND STRIKES AGAIN

You have made a career out of escaping from prisons. You've taken an early vacation from three others before this. You don't think Alcatraz will be any different.

The first time, you were just 16. You stole a car for fun and got sent to county jail. You escaped by distracting the guard at dinner. Then you hit him over the head with his own gun.

You stayed out of trouble for a while, but at age 20 you were caught in an armed robbery. This time you were sent to federal prison in Kansas. There, your cellmate was an older guy who recognized your intelligence and keen skills.

Turn the page.

Clancy helped you better understand how to case a prison and figure out escape routes. He taught you how to time the guards on their rounds, watch them interact, and learn which ones aren't too smart. He told you how to figure out which ones have a big ego that you can use to your advantage. You should make friends with the old-timers so you can learn their secrets. He even taught you about prison architecture.

You escaped that prison within the year. But you were caught robbing a store a couple years later, returning to prison once again. This time you escaped and lived in hiding for years, fooling the authorities. When they finally caught you, the arresting agent advised the judge to send you to a place where escape would be impossible. That meant one thing: You went to The Rock.

"I guarantee you won't escape *that!*" the judge said.

You took it as a challenge.

You haven't been here long when another prisoner recognizes you. Kelly approaches you in the yard and tells you he was in that Kansas prison when you broke out. "I know a way out of here," he says. He wants to team up with you to escape from Alcatraz.

To team up with Kelly, turn to page 46.
To go it alone, turn to page 48.

It's cold in the yard today, and Kelly isn't wearing his jacket. Tough guy. Yeah, you remember him.

"All right," you say. You glance around to make sure nobody is listening. "What's this big secret you have?"

"Buddy of mine worked in maintenance some years ago," Kelly says. "He took a fan out of a ceiling shaft above our cell block. He was supposed to repair it and put it back. But you know how things go—he got pulled off on another job. That fan never went back in."

"So the shaft is open," you say.

"All we have to do is get up there. From there, we can get on the roof."

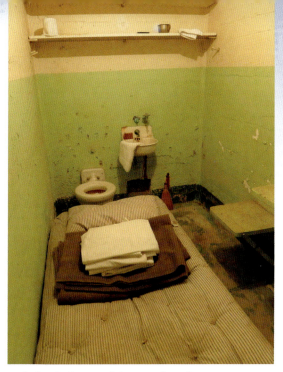

Cells in Blocks B and C were 5 by 9 feet
(1.5 by 2.7 m).

That night, you stare at the ceiling in your
cell and imagine the open shaft. How can you get
up there? You can study the guards for a couple
weeks and try to figure out their patterns. Maybe
they'll give you a clue. On the other hand, maybe
there's a way to dig out of your cell.

To study the guards, turn to page 50.
To dig your way out, turn to page 53.

You never know who you can trust, especially in prison. You're already uncomfortable with the attention from Kelly. The guards notice every friendship, every suspicious activity . . . every move you make.

"Sorry," you tell Kelly, "I'm not looking for trouble right now."

Over the next few weeks, you case every inch of the prison. You watch the guards during mealtime. You study the bathroom and shower. In the yard, you scan the guard towers, gates, and wall. You watch the mail delivery, laundry collection, trash cleanup, and headcount procedures.

You are assigned a job in the laundry room. The big machines fill the air with hot steam. The smell of cleaning chemicals is strong.

Many convicts use the laundry to pass messages and illegal items. You quickly learn who has power in Alcatraz. And one person seems to have a lot of friends—and a lot of secrets. That person is Kelly.

You're learning a lot. But so far, you haven't found any way to get out.

"OK," you tell Kelly one night. "I give up. What's your secret?"

Kelly tells you about an open air shaft behind the walls of your cells. It leads to the maintenance corridor above the cell block. If you can get to the air shaft, you can use it to climb to freedom. What will you do?

To join forces with Kelly, turn to page 53.
To keep trying on your own, turn to page 55.

Every day, every waking moment, you keep one eye on the guards around you. When they change shifts, you listen to what they say. When they pass your cell, you notice what they're looking at. You check which ones are armed with guns and which are not.

One night after lights out, Lieutenant French pauses in front of your cell and looks in at you. You're lying on the bed trying to ignore him, but he doesn't leave.

"You need something?" you say.

Finally he speaks up. "You're not so bright, you know."

"What?" you say, stunned.

"I see what you're doing. And I'm telling you: I will be ready."

Then he takes a metal baton and raps on each of the bars of your cell. He's listening for any bar that might produce a flatter sound—evidence that it has been tampered with. But all the bars ring true. In the darkness, you see a tiny hint of a smile on his face.

Turn the page.

At its height, Alcatraz housed 302 prisoners.

"Good night," he says.

Your skin turns cold. You think back and realize that French has been watching you as much as you've been watching him. Your reputation as an escape artist has worked against you. French is smart. You almost respect him. If you met on the outside, you might even be friends.

The guard's footsteps echo down the cell block. His baton raps against more bars. You lie in the dark and listen. It sinks in that you can't risk an escape. Not while Lieutenant French is here. And he's going to be here a long time.

THE END

To follow another path, turn to page 9.
To learn more about Alcatraz, turn to page 103.

You tell Kelly that you think there's a way to dig out of the cells. But you need a good tool. Then you sit and wait patiently for something to happen.

One day in the yard, Kelly slips you something wrapped in cloth. Back in your cell, you carefully open it up. It's a drill bit. He really is well-connected.

That night, you use the drill bit to scrape around the air vent under your sink. The vent leads to the air shaft. Chunks of concrete start falling off. Each night you work for a couple hours while Kelly keeps a lookout. When a guard enters the cell block, Kelly gives two quick taps on the bars of his cell. That's your signal to move clothes in front of the grate and get quickly into bed.

Turn the page.

Before long, you have chipped all the way through the wall in a rectangle around the grate. You can pull it out. You give Kelly the drill bit to work on his own vent.

While you're waiting for him to chip around his vent, you decide you should go up and investigate that air shaft. The only problem is, the guards check the cells every hour. Can you crawl through the opening in your cell, climb up the maintenance corridor, find the open air shaft, inspect it, and get back to your cell before the guards come around again?

If you believe you can do it, turn to page 58.
To try to come up with a safer way, turn to page 60.

You can't trust anyone, not even Kelly. Besides, you have a plan. From your job in the laundry, you can steal a guard uniform one piece at a time. Once you have it all together, you can wait for the right time during your shift to slip out. Your uniform will get you onto a ferry back to the mainland.

After watching the guards for weeks, you pick your target. The one named Giles is not very bright. You've seen him forget to lock a gate, miscount prisoners on shift, and get confused about where he was supposed to be. Other guards make fun of him. Lieutenant French picks on him. He could be an easy target.

You hide the uniform behind a stack of bleach barrels. Once you have it ready, it's time to make your move on Giles. You start by letting him know you have noticed how Lieutenant French treats him.

Turn the page.

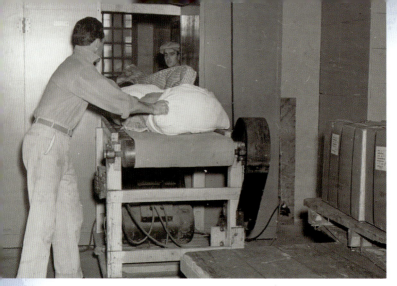
Workers at the Alcatraz laundry washed clothes for military bases in the San Francisco Bay area.

"I thought you ordered the cleanout line cleared today," you say one afternoon. "I guess French overruled you again."

Another day you mention how the big laundry carts need repairs. Several of the wheels are going bad. "Didn't you tell French about it?"

"I told him," Giles says. "He says to wait. He thinks he's smarter than everyone."

"He ought to listen to you more," you say.

It takes months, but Giles starts to think of you as an ally. Finally, you take a chance and ask Giles to make a copy of the gate key. You'll escape in your stolen uniform while French is on duty. It will make French look bad. Maybe he'll even be fired.

The laundry machines hum and clank while Giles chews his cheek, thinking. Does he hate French enough to frame him?

"Lieutenant French *is* a jerk," he says. "But I can't do that. I'll tell you what I *will* do, though. I'll wait until tomorrow to search the supply area. You might want to make sure I don't find anything."

Well, you think, *There's no getting off The Rock today*. But at least your friendship with Giles saved you from solitary.

THE END

To follow another path, turn to page 9.
To learn more about Alcatraz, turn to page 103.

It shouldn't be hard to get up there and back in less than an hour. All you are doing is checking to see if the shaft really is open and how big it is.

After the guard passes through the cell block, you jump out of bed. As quietly as possible, you slide out the grate. You shimmy through the narrow opening one shoulder at a time. Then you reach back into the cell and pull the grate back in place.

You feel your way in the dark until you find a set of pipes, and you begin to climb up. At the top of the third floor cell block, you step onto the landing. Craning your neck to peer up, you scan the ceiling shafts. They're all dark and full. But then through one shaft you see a cloudy moonlit sky. Jackpot!

Time is running short, so you quickly descend the pipes. When you push your cell vent out of the way, it clatters onto the floor. The sound echoes in the cell block.

Just as you are hurrying to climb back into your cell, a light shines in your eyes. "What's going on here?" the guard says. You close your eyes and picture that open shaft. That memory is as close as you'll ever get to seeing the night sky again.

THE END

To follow another path, turn to page 9.
To learn more about Alcatraz, turn to page 103.

Right now there is something more important than sneaking out. You have to hide the dug-out concrete around the grate in your cell. You've been keeping clothes in front of it, but it won't be long before the guards get suspicious.

At dinner one night, you lean close and whisper to Kelly, "Start requesting magazines from the library. Lots of them." Your plan is to tear out pages from the magazines, cut the pages into strips, and mix them with glue and concrete dust to make paper-mache. From that, you can make a fake model of the concrete and grate.

"You're a genius," Kelly says.

You also order painting supplies. Since you both have good behavior records, you're allowed to paint pictures in your cell. Of course, you have other plans for the paint.

You mix the paper-mache in your sink and build a fake vent grate. You paint it to match the mint green wall of your cell. You remove the real grate and slide it into the maintenance corridor behind your cell. The fake one fits perfectly. Next, you make paper-mache dummy heads and paint them to look like your and Kelly's heads.

The final step is to find a way to get off the island. Through your job in the laundry, you learn that an inmate named Papa is a powerful gangster. He has connections on the outside. People say he can make things happen.

But is it smart to get another person involved in your plan?

To ask Papa for help, turn to page 62.
To find your own way with Kelly, turn to page 65.

Wide concrete steps runs along one side of the exercise yard. Inmates call them the "bleachers." The longer you have been inside, and the more powerful you are, the higher you are allowed to sit. Nobody would dare climb too high up the bleachers—not unless they wanted to get killed.

Papa sits at the very top. One cool spring day you ask for permission to come up.

You do have a bit of a friendship with Papa. You have passed contraband for him in the laundry. Still, you are nervous until Papa's messenger comes down and says it's okay.

You climb the bleachers and thank the gangster for letting you up. You tell him your situation: You have a way to get out, but you need help. You describe the plan. You assure Papa that you have been extremely careful. It will work.

Prisoners spent as little as an hour a week in the prison yard.

Papa agrees. You have proved yourself to be cunning and trustworthy. He says he can get a boat into the water outside the prison. You have to be ready when he gives the word.

More than a month passes. Then suddenly you get the word: Tonight is the night!

Turn the page.

Anxious, you lay in bed while the guard does his first count of the evening. After he leaves the cell block, you place your dummy head on the pillow and stuff clothes under the blanket. You slip into the maintenance corridor and replace the paper grate.

Next door, Kelly is still finishing digging out his grate. Unlike you, he hasn't gotten out yet. And there's a problem: An extra bar reinforces the concrete around his vent.

To help Kelly get his grate out, turn to page 68.
To go without him, turn to page 70.

One night while cutting ads out of a sporting magazine, an article catches your eye. It is about body surfing. It gives you an idea. A supply boat ferries back to the mainland every night. You can body surf behind it and get to the coast.

Kelly steals a long coil of rope from the maintenance shop. You both place your dummy heads on your pillows after lights out, slip out of your cells, and climb through the open air vent onto the roof.

Though it is foggy, you can see the moon flash through moving clouds. It has been a long time since you have been outside at night. The sight thrills you.

There's no time to admire the view, though. You and Kelly climb down to the dock. Workers are loading the supply boat. You wait.

Turn the page.

When the boat is loaded, you slip under the dock and toss your rope over the ship's railing. Kelly grabs the other end. As the boat pulls away, you both lean forward. You skim along the surface behind the boat.

There are nearly a dozen species of sharks in the San Francisco Bay, including Great Whites.

As you near the mainland, you release the rope and swim into a cove. On the road above, you walk until you find an unlocked car parked in an apartment parking lot.

The first hint of dawn sets the parking lot aglow. You feel a thrill of freedom as you hotwire the car. That's when you hear tires on the pavement.

"Get down!" Kelly whispers. "It's a cop!"

But it's too late. The police car's red and blue lights flash on, and a voice comes over a loud speaker: "Get out and put your hands up!"

It looks like you are going back to The Rock.

THE END

To follow another path, turn to page 9.
To learn more about Alcatraz, turn to page 103.

The smart thing to do is leave. You know this. But your emotions get the better of you. You can't bring yourself to ditch Kelly.

You wrap your hand around the exposed bar. You pull with all your strength, and it bends toward you. You push it back toward Kelly, then pull it back toward you. You repeat this several times, your hands blistering. Do it enough times, and the bar will snap. But how many times?

You rest while Kelly takes over bending the bar back and forth. He grunts and curses, and you whisper at him to shut up. When a guard passes for the hourly count, Kelly gets back in bed. You hold your breath as the guard passes your dummy head. It fools him. He doesn't give it a second look.

Finally you decide you have to go. The boat will not wait all night. "I'm sorry," you tell him. The look on Kelly's face is enough to make you hesitate. But you really have to go.

You slip easily outside and swim out into the dark water. You've lost at least an hour helping Kelly, and you hope the boat will still be there. You swim toward where it is supposed to be.

You swim farther. You're shivering. You should have seen the boat by now. Gradually it sinks in that it has left. You missed your chance.

THE END

To follow another path, turn to page 9.
To learn more about Alcatraz, turn to page 103.

That boat will not wait long for you. You need to go—now.

"I'll tell them to wait for you," you say to Kelly. But you both know this is a lie. As you climb the pipes toward the top of the building, you hear Kelly crying in his cell. It feels crushing. But you have no choice. If you want to get away, you have to be selfish.

Once outside, a guard tower sweeps its powerful search light along the beach. You lay in some brush and hide the best you can. The light moves smoothly past.

You don't have to swim very far before you see a small blue light flicker three times. That's the signal. You call out, and a motor croaks to life in the black night. It draws near, and a man reaches down to pull you out of the water.

There are two men on the boat. You shiver in a blanket as the boat motors quietly toward the mouth of the bay. As you pass under the Golden Gate Bridge, the captain guns the engine. Wind blows past your face and a wake spools out behind you. By the time the sun rises, you are far out to sea, no land in sight.

THE END

To follow another path, turn to page 9.
To learn more about Alcatraz, turn to page 103.

Chapter 4

CAN THE MECHANIC FIX THIS?

You grew up on a farm. You and your younger brother and sisters worked on everything from tractors and cars to power tools and boilers. You can fix just about *anything*—and you can build anything, too. You and your family were poor but busy and happy.

It was a good life, but it was a hard life too. Everything had to go right in order to pay your bills and have enough to eat. And when the crops went bad two years in a row, things were definitely not going right. You didn't have enough corn to feed your livestock, much less sell. Bills added up, and your family was hungry.

Turn the page.

When the bank repossessed the farm, you moved to a one-bedroom apartment in the city. Your dad had a hard time finding a job. He died a year later—from shame, you always thought.

Finally, you found a job in an auto shop. You made good money, and it felt good to help pay for rent and groceries. But one day, things turned bad again. Two men came into the shop front; one of them had a gun. "Give me all the cash in the drawer," the other one said.

The men did not see you in the back office, but you saw them. It made you angry that these men would just take what they didn't earn. Meanwhile, your hardworking family starves. While your boss took the money out of the drawer, you hit the gunman in the arm. The gun fell to the floor, and you dove after it. So did the other two men.

After a brief fight, the gun went off. One of the men was shot and killed.

You were arrested and sent to trial for your involvement. The judge wanted to make an example of you. You were convicted and sent to Alcatraz.

Every day you think about your mom and siblings. It hurts you that you can't help them. If you could get out, you'd flee to another country and change your identity. You'd find a job and send money home to your family.

To take a job in the prison library, turn to page 76.
To take a job in the maintenance shop, turn to page 78.

Library workers get to push the cart of books and magazines around the cell block. You bring prisoners their reading material. Sometimes, you also pass secret messages. Working in the library is a good way to learn things.

It doesn't take long to notice that there are two brothers on the cell block who pass a lot of contraband back and forth. John and Jeff Bishop tuck the notes into different books that they take turns borrowing. Of course, you mind your own business.

One day at the end of your shift, a well-dressed guard asks you if you've seen any messages or other contraband on the job. His name is Lieutenant French.

"No, sir," you tell him.

"Well, keep an eye out," French says, winking.

The average prison sentence at Alcatraz was eight years.

If you turn in someone who is passing notes, you can earn privileges. You can even get time taken off your sentence.

If you tell the guard about the Bishop brothers, turn to page 80.

If you warn the brothers to be careful, turn to page 82.

You've spent your whole life fixing things. It only makes sense to take a job in the maintenance shop.

Working with you in the shop is another worker named John Bishop. Bishop has been in Alcatraz for a long time. He has a reputation for violence. He is dangerous and unpredictable. You mind your own business and try not to talk to him. But one day you notice him staring at you while you're repairing a hair clipper from the barbershop.

"What?" you say.

"You're good with machines," he says.

"Pretty good. Why?" You realize he has been watching you a lot lately. When he steps closer, you start to worry.

But instead of attacking you, he whispers, "Could you convert the motor in one of those electric razors?"

"Convert it into what?" you ask.

"A drill."

You can do this. It wouldn't be too hard—if you were on the outside. In here? Who knows.

To tell him you can do it, turn to page 84.
To keep minding your own business, turn to page 86.

For the next couple weeks, you track how many messages go back and forth between the Bishop brothers. You even find a razor blade in a book. The next time Lieutenant French asks, you detail how many notes are passing between them. You looked at one, and it was a map of the prison. French nods. He sits quietly for a moment, thinking, then gets on the phone and begins to dial a number.

"You can go," he says. Another guard escorts you back to your cell.

After dinner that night, you and the other prisoners return to the cell block. But something is going on. Jeff Bishop's cell, which is next to yours, is open. Lieutenant French, two other guards, and the warden are standing before it.

Bishop's bed and books are lying in a messy heap in the hall. One of the guards holds a sharpened spoon handle and a razor blade. The spoon handle could be a weapon or a digging tool—or both.

Bishop looks at you with cold eyes; he knows what you did. You realize you have made a terrible mistake. He and his brother will be punished—they'll go to solitary for many months for their foiled escape plan. But then they will return to the cell block. You will never be safe from them. Even if the warden is extremely generous about cutting down your sentence, you can't get out soon enough. You'll be dead.

THE END

To follow another path, turn to page 9.
To learn more about Alcatraz, turn to page 103.

The next day as you push the cart past John Bishop's cell, you pause. "French has heat on you," you whisper. Bishop nods slightly and goes back to his reading.

Days later, Jeff Bishop sits by you at dinner. His brother told him what you said. He thanks you. Then he lowers his voice and says, "We have a way out. But we need someone who can build and fix things."

You don't hesitate. "I'm in," you say.

He gives a small smile. Days later he sits with you at lunch again. "Can you make a raft?"

Out of things found in the prison? The next few days you think about it.

If John Bishop can steal enough raincoats from the supply closet in the maintenance shop, maybe you can make a raft.

The New Industries building was a two-story building. The laundry room was on the upper floor. Industrial work, such as sewing clothing or making shoes, took place downstairs.

But does French still have heat on the Bishop brothers? Maybe it's not safe to get involved.

To tell the boys you can make a raft, turn to page 88.

To keep your distance for now, turn to page 90.

"I can make just about anything," you boast.

A week later, John's brother Jeff slides a cloth bundle to you around the front of your cells. You pull it in and turn your light out to avoid detection as you unwrap the cloth. Inside it are the clippers. There's also a long, sharp drill bit.

Your breath catches. It's illegal to have this in your cell. If you're caught, it will be a world of punishment. But your breath is short for another reason too. Maybe you can escape!

That night, working with no light, you convert the motor. By splitting the power cord to your desk lamp, you rig an electrical arc into a homemade welding torch. Using that, you attach the bit to the motor.

You pass it back to Jeff. But when he sits next to you at lunch the next day, he has bad news.

"We need a bigger drill," he says.

Apparently, he can get out of his cell. Behind the cells, he can get to an air shaft with bars across the top. But the drill wasn't strong enough to get through them.

You think about it. A bigger drill could probably work. On the other hand, if you could get up there, you might be able to find another way through.

To suggest converting a vacuum motor to a drill, turn to page 93.

To ask if you can get up there to take a look, turn to page 95.

"Nah," you say, and walk away. You're not going to get involved in this, whatever it is.

"Suit yourself," he says.

Things are normal for a few months. Then one morning during roll call, something happens. From the end of the corridor, you hear Lieutenant French bark, "Again!"

You look down the cell block, but you can't tell what's going on. Soon it becomes clear though. Two prisoners are missing. One of them is Jeff Bishop, whose cell is right next to yours.

The warden comes. Everyone is locked up. Later you learn that both Bishop brothers have tunneled out of their cells. They are no longer on the island.

A view from a guard station. Cell Block B is on the left and Cell Block C is on the right.

You can't believe it. Everyone said The Rock could not be broken. But they did it. You are excited for them. But at the same time a feeling of despair fills your gut.

You could have been with them.

THE END

To follow another path, turn to page 9.
To learn more about Alcatraz, turn to page 103.

You let the brothers know your plan. John Bishop will need to steal as many raincoats as he can get. You will get to work mixing a strong glue in your sink.

The brothers teach you how to tunnel out of your cell through the air vent in the back, like they have done. The concrete is loose and rotten.

Over the next few weeks, John Bishop steals raincoats. When he goes in for his shift in the shop, he is not wearing one. While he's working, the guards on duty change. When he finishes his shift, he pulls out a raincoat and wears it back to his cell. The new guard assumes he wore it in.

At night, you sneak through your air vent into the corridor where the coats are hidden. There, you carefully cut them apart and glue the parts together to shape two long pontoons.

When you finish the raft, the brothers tell you they want to go—tonight. You have dug holes in your wall. You have a huge raft hidden in the corridor. Staying is risky.

But there is a good reason to wait. The raft is large and will take a lot of air to pump up. If you have to blow it up with your lungs, it could take an hour—maybe longer. With more time, you could fashion a pump out of something. Then you could pump up the raft and get out on the water faster. Once you're on the outside, every minute is precious.

To convince the brothers to wait, turn to page 97.
To take your chances tonight, turn to page 100.

The Bishop brothers agree to hold off—at least for a little while.

While working in the library, you learn that some inmates are planning to fight their way out of the prison. This is bad news. There is almost no chance they will succeed. And afterward, it's going to result in searches of the prison. The Bishop boys have weapons and tools in their cells, and no time to get rid of them. They have even dug tunnels.

They decide they have no choice but to try to get out during the riot.

The next morning, you step to the front of your cell for the morning head count. As Lietenant French walks past the cell of a con named Stinky, Stinky stabs him with something. French screams and crumples to the ground.

Suddenly the cell block is a frenzy of violence. Prisoners are attacking guards with homemade daggers. Stinky gets ahold of French's gun and starts to shoot. The guards on the second floor open fire.

Turn the page.

Prisoners who misbehaved could be sent to solitary confinement.

Gun smoke fills the air. The alarm is going off. Guards and inmates are lying on the floor bleeding. You follow Stinky through the kitchen to the trash burner. He has French's keys, and unlocks the door.

Outside, you begin to climb a chain link fence. Stinky is laughing. He thinks he's made it. Just then, gun fire erupts behind you. The fence shakes. You look at Stinky. He looks surprised that they got him. His legs slip, but his fingers stay curled in the fence.

You keep climbing. But a moment later bullets tear into your own back, and you fall.

THE END

To follow another path, turn to page 9.
To learn more about Alcatraz, turn to page 103.

"I saw vacuum motors going into the shop for repairs," you whisper to Jeff. "I need one."

Jeff tells you how to use a sharpened spoon handle to dig out your own vent. That way you can get into the maintenance corridor like he does.

It takes a couple weeks of digging at night, but you get through. When you do, the stolen vacuum motor is in the corridor waiting for you. Using the same method as before, you convert it into a drill.

When it's ready, Jeff slips out of his cell. Suddenly, there's a loud noise—a loud noise that sounds a lot like a vacuum cleaner.

Jeff turns off the motor, but it's too late. Everyone heard it. Guards are rushing onto the cell block. They find Jeff's hole, and they find Jeff crawling back into his cell.

Turn the page.

In 1962 prisoners attempted to escape by loosening the air vents in their cells. One of the tools used was a drill made with a vacuum cleaner motor.

It's over. Jeff wastes no time in telling the guards everything. As you are locked into solitary, you think of your mother. Once again, you have failed to help her.

THE END

To follow another path, turn to page 9.
To learn more about Alcatraz, turn to page 103.

"A bigger drill might be too loud," you say. "But maybe I can get through the bars another way. I just need to get up there and see."

Jeff gives you the drill bit. You use it to dig out the concrete around the air vent under the sink. In a couple weeks, you get the grate out.

You climb through the hole and up to the top of the cell block. Jeff shows you the air vent, and you shimmy up inside. You inspect the bars. You realize there are screws holding the circular grill in the shaft. You take the drill bit and dig into the concrete around the ring. It crumbles, just like the concrete around the air vent in your cell.

Soon you reach a screw behind the circular grill. Using the drill bit, you're able to hack at it until it breaks. You repeat the process on the other side.

Turn the page.

You climb back down. "I broke two of the screws," you tell Jeff. "There are two more—we can break those when we are ready to go."

"We need a raft if we want to get across the bay," Jeff says.

You have a plan for that too. "Tell John to steal as many raincoats as he can from the supply closet in the maintenance shop. Hide them in the corridor behind my cell."

Soon, a pile of raincoats grows behind your cell. Every night, you sneak back there and cut the raincoats apart. You mix a strong homemade glue in your sink. In time, you build a two-pontoon raft. What you need now is something to inflate it.

Go to page 97.

You and the Bishop brothers are talking in the yard. Seagulls cry overhead. Clouds move quickly past in the heavy wind.

"I have an idea," you say. You have been watching a couple men play guitar out of the corner of your eye. "I'm going to order an accordion."

"Those things sound terrible," Jeff Bishop says.

"That's not the point," you say.

You order the instrument and practice playing it each night after dinner. You want the guards to think you really love music. There's no other reason for ordering an accordion.

Then one night you turn out your lights and climb through your air vents. You carry the accordion with you. The two brothers drag the raft and the sheets from their bed.

Turn the page.

At the top of the air shaft in the ceiling, you use the drill bit to chip away the final two screws in the circular grill of bars. You push it out over the top, being careful not to let it clang on the roof. Then you use the sheets to climb down the side of the building.

At the beach, you quickly remove part of the bellows and convert the accordion into a pump. What little music the instrument makes as you pump is lost to the wind and waves. The raft quickly fills—first one pontoon, then the other.

Using bookshelves as paddles, you move easily across the bay. When you near the shore, you puncture the raft so it sinks. The authorities will find it and assume it sank with you on board. You hope they will think you drowned.

A view of the main cell block. In Alcatraz's 29-year history, 36 men were involved in 14 escape attempts. Two men tried to escape twice.

Your patience has paid off. With the head start you got, you will be far away before they even realize you're gone. You and the brothers split up. You hitchhike to Canada. When you get there, you'll get a job. As soon as you can, you'll start sending money home to your family.

THE END

To follow another path, turn to page 9.
To learn more about Alcatraz, turn to page 103.

That night, you and the Bishop brothers all break out through your loose ventilation grates. You climb to the top of the cell block and into the empty air shaft. You pull the bulky raft up behind you. Soon, you are all outside on the rooftop. The ocean air smells great! It smells like freedom.

You toss your raft over the side of the building. Using bedsheets from your cells, you climb down to the ground. The three of you drag the raft to the shore, where you take turns blowing into it. You were right—it takes a long time. Even after half an hour, it still looks flat.

Finally, you decide it's close enough. You push your flabby boat out into the waves and climb in. Using a bookshelf from your cell, you paddle out into the fog.

The raft begins taking on water. Even the smallest waves splash over the sagging sides.

You bail out as much as you can with your hands, but it's a losing battle. The raft is going slower and slower with the extra weight. And the water is over your knees as you kneel in the bottom. The brothers whisper among themselves. Then they turn to you.

"There's too much weight in here," John Bishop says.

They plan to throw you overboard. Instead of letting them, you jump out. It won't help them anyway. They might make it farther than you. But you're all going to end up at the bottom of the bay.

THE END

To follow another path, turn to page 9.
To learn more about Alcatraz, turn to page 103.

Chapter 5

THE ESCAPE-PROOF ROCK

The earliest known occupants of the island that came to be known as Alcatraz were indigenous peoples known as Ohlone. The Ohlone sent their criminals to live on the island in isolation.

In 1759 a Spanish explorer named Juan Manuel Diaz discovered the island and named it "La Isla de los Alcatraces," or "The Island of Pelicans." Apparently the island was home to many brown pelicans.

The Spanish built some buildings while they were there. The land passed to the United States after the Mexican-American War (1846–1848). They built a fortress and armed it during the Civil War (1861–1865).

The first prison wasn't built until 1867. Then the U.S. Department of Justice took over in 1933. It became a federal prison the following year.

Alcatraz Federal Prison was where the most dangerous criminals were sent. It housed such notorious men as Al Capone (known as "Scarface"), George Barnes ("Machine Gun Kelly"), Bumpy Johnson, and James "Whitey" Bulger. Its isolated island location, as well as the most modern high-security reinforcements, gave it the reputation of being considered escape-proof.

That reputation didn't stop prisoners from trying. During its 29 years as a federal penitentiary, there were 14 escape attempts. The official line is that none of them were successful. Not everyone agrees with that.

Alcatraz was closed as a prison on March 21, 1963. It was deemed too expensive to keep up. Later it reopened as a museum. Visitors can ride a boat to the island and tour the buildings and hear stories about life on The Rock.

In 1962 convicts used fake heads made with soap, toilet paper, paint, and real human hair to fool prison guards into thinking they were still in their cells.

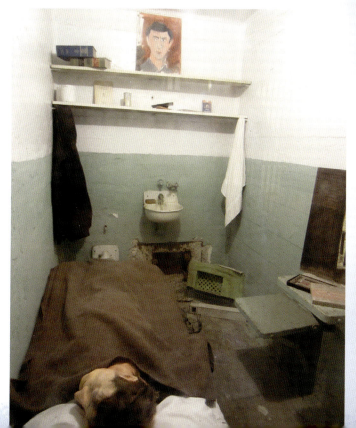

REAL ESCAPE ATTEMPTS

April 27, 1936: A prisoner working at the garbage incinerator makes a run for it. He was shot trying to climb the fence.

December 16, 1937: Two prisoners filed through iron bars and got out. They are believed to have drowned in stormy waters.

May 23, 1938: Three men killed a guard with a hammer in the woodshop. Two were shot and killed, and the other man surrendered on the roof.

January 13, 1939: Five inmates escaped from their cells and made it to the shore. A guard spotted them and opened fire, killing one man and wounding another. The others were taken alive.

May 21, 1941: Four inmates took several guards hostage. But they could not saw through the tool-proof bars to escape before being re-captured.

September 15, 1941: An inmate slipped away from the guards while working on garbage duty. He started to swim for freedom but gave up.

April 14, 1943: Four inmates cut through the bars in an industrial room. They collected cans to use as flotation devices. They attacked and tied up two guards before escaping out the window. The guards managed to get loose and alert the prison. One prisoner was killed, two were recovered, and one remained missing. He hid in a nearby cave, but after two days snuck back in the same window he had escaped from.

August 7, 1943: An inmate working in the laundry escaped and made it to the two security fences. He had stolen wire cutters, but they didn't work, and he had to climb both fences. He fell from the second fence and injured his back. He was captured.

July 31, 1945: A prisoner stole an army uniform from the laundry and got on board a government boat. But when he was discovered to be missing through a headcount, the boat was held at Angel Island, where he was caught.

May 2—4, 1946: Six prisoners staged a violent riot, later named the Battle of Alcatraz. They attacked guards and got into the weapons room. There, they got keys to the recreation yard. But they ended up in a bloody fight. They took two guards hostage. The U.S. Marines were called in and helped the guards kill three of the convicts. The prisoners had already killed the two hostages and injured 17 other guards. The three surviving inmates who started the riot were convicted of murder, and two of them were sentenced to death. Clarence Carnes, who was only 19 years old, was given a second life sentence on top of the one he already was serving.

July 23, 1956: A prisoner escaped from his job at the dock. He hid in the rocks at the shore and tried to build a raft out of driftwood. He was soon caught.

September 29, 1958: Two convicts escaped while working on garbage detail. One was caught in the water. The other drowned, and his body was discovered two weeks later.

June 11, 1962: Frank Morris, John Anglin, and his brother Clarence Anglin had reputations of escaping prison. They worked together to escape. Each dug away the concrete surrounding their cell's air vents, gaining access to a utility corridor behind the wall. They made fake walls and grills out of paper-mache to hide their work.

They also made paper-mache heads to leave on their pillows. The heads made it look like they were still in their cells while they were outside building a raft.

Another convict, Alan West, tricked the guards into hanging sheets over the third-floor railing. He told them it was to keep dust from falling while he cleaned up there. Morris and the Anglins used the sheets to hide their raft.

On the night of their escape, West could not get out of his cell. His "door" was not ready, and the other three left him behind. They climbed to the top of the cell block and into an air vent that had had its fan removed. The men were never seen again.

A gangster named Bumpy Johnson was rumored to have arranged for a boat to pick them up. Years later, a photo surfaced of two men who looked a lot like the Anglin brothers. The men were in Brazil. But nothing ever came of it. To this day, many believe the men escaped. Alcatraz officials said they died crossing the bay. But nobody knows for sure.

December 16, 1962: Two prisoners slipped out a kitchen window and tried to swim to freedom. One was found on a small rocky island not far away. The other was discovered near the Golden Gate Bridge. He had hypothermia and was in shock. Both were returned to Alcatraz.

OTHER PATHS TO EXPLORE

◈ Everyone loves a good escape story. But the men on Alcatraz were violent criminals. Does that make it harder to root for them? Why or why not?

◈ Do you think any of the men who really attempted to escape from Alcatraz were successful? Why or why not?

◈ A successful escape from Alcatraz means getting out of your cell, out of the prison, across the bay, and far away from San Francisco. Make up your own escape story. How would you do each of these parts?

READ MORE

Braun, Eric. *Escape From Alcatraz: The Mystery of the Three Men Who Escaped From The Rock.* North Mankato, MN: Capstone Press, 2017.

Burling, Alexis. *Occupying Alcatraz: Native American Activists Demand Change.* Minneapolis: Essential Library, an imprint of Abdo Publishing, 2017.

Evans, Christine. *Escaping Alcatraz.* Mankato, MN: The Childs World, 2018.

INTERNET SITES

Alcatraz History.
https://www.alcatrazhistory.com

Federal Bureau of Prisons: Alcatraz.
https://www.bop.gov/about/history/alcatraz.jsp

National Parks Service: Alcatraz Island.
https://www.nps.gov/alca/learn/historyculture/us-penitentiary-alcatraz.htm

INDEX

COULD YOU ESCAPE THE PARIS CATACOMBS?

BY MATT DOEDEN

CAPSTONE PRESS
a capstone imprint

You Choose Books are published by Capstone Press
1710 Roe Crest Drive, North Mankato, Minnesota 56003
www.capstonepub.com

Library of Congress Cataloging-in-Publication Data
Names: Doeden, Matt, author.
Title: Could you escape the Paris catacombs? : an interactive survival
  adventure / by Matt Doeden.
Description: North Mankato, Minnesota : Capstone Press, [2020] | Series: You
  choose: can you escape? | Summary: Your survival depends on making the
  right choices at key moments when you are lost in the catacombs of Paris.
Identifiers: LCCN 2019008531| ISBN 9781543573947 (hardcover) | ISBN
  9781543575620 (paperback) | ISBN 9781543573985 (ebook pdf)
Subjects: LCSH: Plot-your-own stories. | CYAC: Catacombs—Fiction. |
  Survival—Fiction. | Plot-your-own stories. | Paris (France)—Fiction. |
  France—Fiction.
Classification: LCC PZ7.D692 Co 2020 | DDC [Fic]—dc23
LC record available at https://lccn.loc.gov/2019008531

Editorial Credits
Mari Bolte, editor; Bobbie Nuytten, designer; Eric Gohl, media researcher:
Laura Manthe, premedia specialist

Photo Credits
Alamy: Album, 92, Edward Westmacott, 36, Hemis, 46; Bridgeman Images:
Archives Charmet/Bibliotheque des Arts Decoratifs, Paris, France, 10, Bibliotheque
Nationale, Paris, France, 85, Photo © The Holbarn Archive, 80, Sputnik/State Russian
Museum, St. Petersburg, Russia, 34; Capstone: 4; Newscom: akg-images, 16, SIPA/
Eric Beracassat, 50; Shutterstock: Alex Guevara, 22, Andrea Izzotti, 6, 89, 105,
FrimuFilms, 29, Ilias Kouroudis, cover (tunnel), back cover, javarman, 76, Novikov
Aleksey, 61, Ravenash, 56, Stas Guk, 71, 72, Steven Bostock, cover (skulls), Viacheslav
Lopatin, 42; SuperStock: age fotostock/Javier Marina, 102, Photononstop, 98

All internet sites appearing in back matter were available and accurate when this book
was sent to press.

Printed and bound in China. P04940

TABLE OF CONTENTS

Rue Froidevaux

Boulevard Raspail

Avenue Denfert-Rochereau

Boulevard Arago

Square Jacques-Antoine

Square Claude-Nicolas-Ledoux

Boulevard Saint-Jacques

Entrance

Avenue du Général Leclerc

Avenue René Coty

Rue de la Tombe Issoire

Rue Hallé

Rue Hallé

Rue Dareau

Rue du Couëdic

Exit

Rue Rémy Dumoncel

500 feet

ABOUT YOUR ADVENTURE

YOU are deep below the streets of Paris, France, in the twisting network of tunnels known as the Paris Catacombs. It's dark and damp. Every footfall echoes off of the cracked walls. Skulls grin at you as your flashlight begins to flicker. Your heart races at the thought of the darkness closing in around you.

A small portion of the tunnels are open to the public. But you went off the grid, in search of the unknown. Can you escape the wild, unmapped depths of the Paris Catacombs? Your choices will guide the story. Will you backtrack or delve deeper? Will you scream for help? Will anyone hear you if you do? Can you find a way out—or will you join the others as a permanent part of the catacombs?

Turn the page to begin your adventure.

Chapter 1

THE CATACOMBS CALL

You've landed in Paris. The city is full of life. People pass you as you stroll down the streets, speaking animatedly to friends or just enjoying the bright sun and fresh air. You're surrounded by historical sites and modern-day marvels. This trip is a dream come true.

But, even here in the open street full of wonder, there's a part of the city you can't stop thinking about. You've heard of this place, but only in whispers. The mystery sparked your interest from the first mention. You've thought about going there and seeing things for yourself for years. You can't miss this opportunity. The Paris Catacombs are calling you from below.

Turn the page.

The underground tunnels, resting place to six million dead, are not a secret, but the air of mystery surrounds them. It's another world and largely unmapped. It's a frontier . . . a massive grave . . . a historical monument. It fills you with equal parts terror and wonder. "Don't go down there alone," people warn. "You may never return." Yet you cannot shake the urge to see it for yourself.

Your footsteps quicken as you start to move through the streets with a purpose. You have to go. You have to explore for yourself. An opening stands before you. The catacombs lie beyond. A trickle of sunlight spills into the opening. It creates a narrow shaft of light that dims, then fades away into pitch blackness. You can hear the distant dripping of water and a low, creaky scraping sound.

You take a breath and step forward into the darkness. A wave of cool, damp air sweeps over you. You pause, waiting for your eyes to adjust to the darkness. "This is it," you whisper. You take another step, then another. You have entered the Catacombs of Paris.

To see the catacombs as a young worker in the late 1700s, turn to page 11.

To explore the catacombs as a modern-day tourist, turn to page 37.

To help rescue of a group of teens lost in the labyrinth, turn to page 77.

Chapter 2

NIGHT SHIFT

The first thing that hits you is the smell. Even before you step foot inside the catacombs, the powerful odor of death and decay is evident. It's almost enough to make you turn around.

"Don't worry," says Luc. This is your first day on the job, but Luc has been doing it for a week. "You'll get used to it. I think I turned about four shades of green on my first day, but now I barely notice it."

It's 1785, and you're a teenager trying to make your way in Paris, one of the greatest cities in the world. It's a strange and fascinating time. The city's graveyards are filled beyond capacity.

Turn the page.

Local authorities have decided that the graveyards will be emptied. The remains of countless millions will be moved to an ancient series of mining tunnels that lie below the city's streets. You've taken a lot of odd jobs since you came to Paris a year ago. But this is by far the strangest.

"It's not a complicated job," Luc explains to you. "Workers above ground dig up the bodies from the old Holy Innocents cemetery. They dump them down a well that leads into the quarry—that's the part of the catacombs where we'll be working. We just stack the bones down below. Simple."

A shudder runs down your spine. "OK, but isn't all of this spooky enough? Why do we only work at night?"

Luc laughs. "I wondered the same thing. But then I thought about it. How do you think the fine, upstanding citizens of Paris would feel about this project? They want to pretend not to know. So we work at night. That way, we don't get so many complaints."

As you make your way down deeper into the quarries, the horror of the situation strikes you. The path is lit with flickering torches and lanterns. The piles of remains seem even creepier.

Workers are stacking bodies onto carts. Then they pile them high along the walls of the quarry's large chambers. The bodies are in various stages of decay. Some of the bones are a thousand years old and browned with age. Eyeless skulls stare at you from every angle.

Turn the page.

The smell is more concentrated here in the tunnels. It makes you retch. When Luc first told you about this job, it sounded interesting. Now it feels like you signed up for a horror story.

"You two, get back to work!" An older, balding man approaches you. "We have corpses coming in by the thousands tonight. I want them stacked on that far wall. Get to it!"

You and Luc work as a team loading the dead onto carts. Some of them are very old. They're nothing but bones wrapped in rags. Others aren't fully decayed yet. Those are the ones that really make your stomach churn. You load and wheel one cart after another. As Luc grabs the feet of yet another body, you grab under the shoulders. You heave it onto a pile. It lands with a sickening crunch. It's all too much.

"I'm going to vomit," you say.

"Don't do it in here!" Luc replies. He points to a nearby passageway. "Go down there. The smell is already unbearable in here. We don't need to add vomit to it."

You put one hand over your mouth while holding a torch in the other. You rush down the tunnel. You don't want to let the other workers hear you heaving, so you follow the tunnel until you're far from earshot. You drop to your hands and knees.

When you're done, you feel dizzy. Your head is swimming, and your stomach is still churning. You should get back before you get in trouble for slacking off. But you fear that if you stand up, you might faint or throw up again.

To get up and go back to work, turn to page 16.
To rest here for a few minutes, turn to page 18.

It's your first day on the job. You've got to get back. Using one arm to brace yourself against the cold wall, you rise to your feet. Immediately, the world begins to spin. Before you realize what's happening, you black out. Your body collapses to the hard stone floor.

Most of the catacombs are more than 100 feet (30.5 meters) below street level.

When you wake up, everything feels fuzzy. You don't know how long you were unconscious. Your torch lies beside you, just barely burning. If it goes out, you'll be in total darkness. You have to get back to the main chamber—now!

You look around. You're at an intersection of tunnels. Which one did you take to get down here? You were in such a rush that you weren't paying much attention. And now the knock on your head has you feeling confused and sluggish.

"Was it that way?" you mumble to yourself, peering down into the darkness. "Yes . . . yes. That way. I think it was that way."

Your torch flickers. The flame is almost out. If you stay still and call for help, the light will last longer. But what if no one hears?

To stay where you are and yell for help, turn to page 19.
To grab the torch and start running, turn to page 24.

You just need a minute or two to catch your breath. The smell in the side tunnel is not as bad as the larger chamber. You sit for a moment to let your turning stomach settle.

That's when something catches your eye. It's a faint orange glow coming from farther down the tunnel. It looks like torchlight, and it appears to be moving. Who would be down here? None of the workers would have a reason to be that deep in the catacombs. And no one else is allowed down here at night.

To investigate the light, turn to page 20.

To return to work, turn to page 21.

"Luc!" you shout. Your voice echoes off of the tunnel walls. "Anyone?"

It takes a few moments before you see a torchlight. To your relief, it's Luc.

"I was just about to give up on you," he says. "I was wheeling the cart back when I heard you call. Feeling better?" He helps you to your feet. "Don't worry, it's happened to all of us."

Luc leads you back to the main part of the quarry. You've got to get back to work if you want to keep your job. There's no time to waste.

Turn to page 21.

Your curiosity gets the best of you. You pick yourself up and start down the tunnel in the direction of the torchlight. You're heading away from the quarry. But as long as you don't take any turns, you feel confident that you can find your way back.

You follow the winding tunnel. The torchlight grows steadily brighter. Finally, you catch up to it.

It's a man holding the torch. He doesn't seem surprised to see you, which seems a little odd.

"I'm Phil," he says. "Come now, the treasure is near. Are you going to help me find it?"

"Treasure?" you ask, confused. "What treasure?"

Phil doesn't seem to hear you. "Come!" he snaps, walking farther down the tunnel. "It's close now. I've never been so close. Let's go!"

To decline Phil's offer, turn to page 23.
To join Phil and search for treasure, turn to page 26.

While you've been sick in the tunnels, the others have been working hard. Some noticed your absence, so you jump right in to help. Stacking the bones still makes you feel ill, but it's not quite as bad as before. Maybe Luc is right. Maybe with time, you'll be able to forget that you're touching corpses.

While some workers just stack remains, others have started crafting the bones into works of art. They carefully arrange them against the walls and into structures. Some start calling this decorated area the ossuary. The ossuary would be beautiful if it wasn't made from human remains.

Night after night, you return to the catacombs. The dead pile grows higher and higher. Millions of bones line the walls.

Turn the page.

The catacomb's tunnels were created when limestone was mined to build the city in as early as the 14th century.

Months later, you're busy at work when you hear that a man is missing. Someone wandered too far into the tunnels and hasn't returned. You flash back to your first day on the job and the terror you felt alone in the dark. You shudder thinking about someone else lost in those tunnels.

To go search for the missing man, turn to page 32.

To stay put and keep working, turn to page 35.

You watch as Phil disappears around a corner. What were you thinking coming down here? Who follows a stranger into the dark? It's time to get back to reality.

You turn to make your way back to the large chamber. But there are so many paths to choose from. What seemed like a straight walk in one direction feels quite different now. How do you get back? You glance at your torch. It's still burning strong, but it won't last forever.

You follow the tunnel that you think is the way out. After a while, you wonder how long you've been walking. It seems like a long time. Did you go the wrong way? Panic begins to set in. If you're lost, there's probably no hope for you. No one—except Phil—knows where you are.

To turn around and try a different tunnel, turn to page 28.
To continue along this tunnel, turn to page 30.

The thought of being trapped down here in the dark is terrifying. You have to go, and you have to go *now*. You pick yourself up and start down the closest tunnel. You start at a brisk walk, but soon you are running.

You round a bend, then another. Nothing looks familiar. You've gone too far. Or—not far enough? This can't be the right tunnel!

You spin around and start in the other direction. Maybe you missed a path. You turn so fast that the torch flickers. Then it dies. You are left in total darkness. You freeze in your tracks, looking for any faint glow of light. You listen for any sound. There's nothing. There's only darkness and silence.

"Help!" you shout. "Anyone! Help me, please!"

The only sound you hear is the echo of your own voice.

Luc probably thinks you gave up and went home. Nobody is going to come looking for you. All you can do is blindly roam the tunnels, hoping to see some light or hear a voice. But in the twisting tunnels of the Paris Catacombs, you know that your odds aren't very good.

THE END

To follow another path, turn to page 9.
To learn more about the Paris Catacombs, turn to page 103.

The word "treasure" catches your interest. What could be more exciting than a treasure hunt? If you found a huge stack of gold, you'd never have to have a horrible job again.

Forgetting Luc and basic common sense, you charge off after Phil. He leads you on a winding path through the catacombs. At times it feels like you're walking in circles, but Phil says he can sense that the treasure is close.

"Any moment now," he mumbles, holding his torch out in front of him. "I can smell it. Can you smell it? It's close."

You trek deeper and deeper into the tunnels. The endless twists and turns make you feel dizzy. Finally, Phil lets out a squeal and takes off running. "It's here! It's here!"

He's surprisingly quick. You do your best to keep up, but you're quickly losing ground. Phil disappears around a corner. By the time you reach it, his light is nowhere to be seen.

You're all alone, deep in the catacombs of Paris. It's cold and damp. And your torch just burned out.

Maybe searching for treasure wasn't your best idea. You wish you could go back in time and make a different choice.

THE END

To follow another path, turn to page 9.
To learn more about the Paris Catacombs, turn to page 103.

Your heart is racing. Everything looks the same! You spin around, looking frantically in both directions. You must have come the wrong way. This can't be right!

You sprint back the way you came, arriving at an intersection of tunnels. Do you go left or right? Your torch flickers. It won't keep burning for much longer. You pick a tunnel and start to run. The thunderous clop-clop of your boots on the stone floor is the only sound you can hear.

Suddenly the floor falls away to nothing. In your panic, you didn't realize that the tunnel opened up into a large mine shaft. You flail your arms. Your fingers grab at the side of the wall, but there's nothing to hold on to. You fall through the open shaft.

Rocks and minerals, including limestone, gypsum, and chalk, were mined from under the city. The Louvre was built with Parisian limestone.

You don't know when you'll hit the bottom. The fall into the darkness seems to take an eternity. You realize that the last thing you will ever see is the faint flickering light of your torch as it hits the stone floor.

THE END

To follow another path, turn to page 9.
To learn more about the Paris Catacombs, turn to page 103.

Just a little farther, you tell yourself. *The way out is straight ahead.* You hope you're right. You know that you're betting with your life. You press forward through the narrow tunnel. Water drips from cracks in the walls. Your torch begins to flicker and dim.

"This is wrong," you say out loud. "What have I done?"

Then you smell it. It's the smell of death. There's a dim glow of light ahead. You quicken your pace and burst out into the main chamber. You never thought you'd be so glad to smell and see thousands of corpses piled together.

"You there," shouts the balding man. "Get back to work!"

You smile and shake your head. "Sorry, I quit," you announce.

You'll apologize to Luc later. Right now, all that matters is getting back above ground. You'll find some other job. You'll have to. You're never stepping foot down here again.

THE END

To follow another path, turn to page 9.
To learn more about the Paris Catacombs, turn to page 103.

You still have nightmares about your first day in the catacombs. You wouldn't wish that on anyone. You're the first to volunteer to search for the missing man. Luc is right behind you. The two of you form a team. Several other men pair up into teams as well.

Luc leads the way down a narrow tunnel. It branches off several times. "I went down this way," he says. "Once. And I didn't go very far. It's very tight and there's loose rock everywhere. But we ought to at least check it out. Watch your footing."

You're just barely able to squeeze through the passageway, which seems more like a crack in the rock than a proper tunnel. You each carry a torch. In the tight quarters, it glows right in your eyes, temporarily blinding you.

As you emerge from one snug section, you spot something ahead. It's the missing man! He's lying on the ground, bleeding from a wound on his head. You call to Luc, and rush over to help.

"He must have bumped his head going through that narrow part," Luc says, looking back the way you came. You peel off your outer shirt and wrap it around the man's wound. He's conscious now, but very groggy.

"What were you doing?" you ask.

"Ghosts. I saw ghosts," the man answers, dazed. "They told me to follow them." That doesn't make any sense to you. You wonder what he really saw. Tales of the dead haunting this place are common, but you've never heard of anyone actually seeing them.

Turn the page.

"I think you've been down here too long, friend," Luc says as he helps the man to his feet. You couldn't agree more. Once you get this worker back to safety, it will be time for you to leave as well. You don't want to be the next one chasing ghosts in the catacombs.

The idea of ghost sightings are popular among those seeking a paranormal experience in the catacombs.

THE END

To follow another path, turn to page 9.
To learn more about the Paris Catacombs, turn to page 103.

You back into a shadow and stand as quietly as you can. Luckily, no one notices you. Several others volunteer to go searching for the missing man. You wish you could help, but you just can't make yourself go into the tunnels again. Once is enough.

The search parties find no trace of the man. He's just . . . gone. With a shudder, you realize that could easily have been you. The catacombs of Paris are no place for adventure. You'll just keep doing your work. There are millions of dead that still need to be stacked.

THE END

To follow another path, turn to page 9.
To learn more about the Paris Catacombs, turn to page 103.

Chapter 3

INTO THE DEPTHS

"Oh look, it's another painting!" says Tonya, rolling her eyes. You playfully tap your older sister on the arm. She's not a fan of art like you and your parents are, and you know she's bored.

"Cut it out," you say. "Mom and Dad have been dreaming about this trip since they were kids."

You do have to admit that art museums are starting to lose their appeal. This is the fifth one you've been to this week. It's not that you don't enjoy seeing classic works of art. But there's more to Paris than da Vinci and Michelangelo.

Your parents stand in front of another painting, deep in thought. They could stare at the same painting for an hour.

Turn the page.

"Come on," you say, dragging Tonya over to where they're standing. "Mom . . . Dad," you begin. They don't even hear you. You clear your throat loudly. "Mom!"

Your mom looks over. "Hmm?" she says.

"We're ready to go," you say. "Would it be OK if the two of us saw some of the city's sights? We could meet you back at the hotel later this evening."

Your mother gives you a long look. "Well, OK," she says. "But stay together. And be back by sunset." She turns back to the painting.

Tonya lets out a little yelp of joy, earning some stern looks from the museum's patrons. The two of you hurry outside. The sun is shining. It's a beautiful day. Three local teenagers stand on a street corner, talking and laughing. One of them waves you over.

"Bonjour. I'm Ines," says a girl with long, straight, black hair. "Did you like the museum?"

Tonya shrugs. "I've seen enough museums," she says. "We're looking to see something else."

Ines smiles. "What did you have in mind?"

Neither of you hesitates. You've talked about them since you found out about this trip. "The catacombs!" you blurt out at the same time.

Ines laughs as her friends gather around. "You could take a tour of the catacombs," she says. "It's a very safe—and legal—way to get a taste of them with the rest of the tourists." Ines winks.

One of the other teens laughs. He's a short boy with wire-rimmed glasses. "Or you can see them the fun way . . . with us!" He extends a hand. "I'm René. This is our friend Peter."

Turn the page.

"If you want to see the *real* catacombs, you've found the right people," Peter brags. "We go exploring there all the time."

"Wait," Tonya says, taking a step back. "I thought people weren't allowed to go down there at all, except with the tours."

Peter laughs. "Of course it's not really legal. But it's not like the catacombs police are down there waiting for us."

Tonya bites her lip. She's not the most adventurous person in the world. You can tell that the idea of breaking the rules is making her nervous. But it fills you with excitement. You just know that if Tonya gave it a chance, you could both have an experience that you'll never forget.

To go with Ines, René, and Peter, go to page 41.
To say no and go on an official tour of the catacombs, turn to page 44.

You know what Tonya is thinking, but this is just an offer you can't refuse. Ines, René, and Peter live here. You're sure they know what they're doing.

"Let's do it!" you blurt out before your sister has a chance to object.

Before heading down, the group stops to grab some gear—flashlights, extra batteries, and snacks. Then Peter leads the group down a dark alleyway. He points toward a manhole tucked against an old stone building.

"That's our way in," Peter says, kneeling down and moving the heavy metal manhole cover. "Not many people know about it. We *cataphiles* keep our entrances as secret as possible." One by one, you slip through the narrow opening and emerge into another world.

Turn the page.

Ines starts an app on her phone. "I use this to keep track of where we've been," she explains. "René is working on building a map of this section of the catacombs."

You walk a little ways on a downward slope. Soon, the only light you can see comes from your flashlights. Everyone has enough batteries for a couple of hours.

The ossuary is decorated with skulls and leg bones. Smaller bones are hidden behind the ossuary walls.

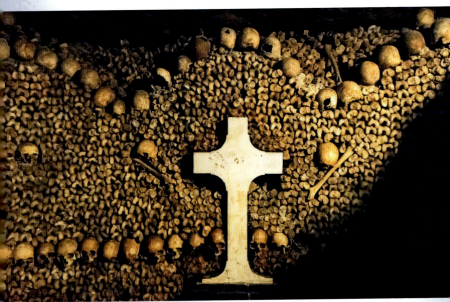

Tonya shivers. "It's cold down here," she says. Her voice sounds strange as it echoes off of the corridor walls. "And these tunnels are so tight."

You agree. You've never been claustrophobic. But down here, you can almost feel the weight of the rock and earth pressing down on you.

The tunnel branches off. "We explored that tunnel yesterday," Ines says, pointing to the left. "There are some cool things to see that way, if you're interested. Or we could go this way," she points to the right. "We haven't mapped any of that yet. We have no idea what we might find. It'll be an adventure!"

To go left and see what the group already discovered, turn to page 49.

To go right and help map a new area, turn to page 52.

The idea of sneaking down into the forbidden parts of the catacombs fills you with excitement. But you look over to see Tonya biting her fingernails—something she always does when she's scared. How much fun would it be if your sister is terrified the whole time? So with a sigh, you politely decline the invitation.

Ines shrugs. "No problem. I'm sure you'll really enjoy a tour. Even the tunnels you're allowed to see are pretty interesting. Have fun!"

"Thanks," you reply with a smile. Already, Tonya seems more at ease. She's not biting her nails anymore, and she looks relieved. "Let's go," you say, pulling her by the arm.

By the time you reach the official entrance to the catacombs, it's mid-afternoon. You barely make it in time for the day's final tour.

You and Tonya follow your guide, a young man named Louis, through the entrance. Half a dozen other tourists follow along behind.

"These were built in the 13th century," Louis explains. "The tunnels stretch for hundreds of miles. Many of the passages remain unmapped to this day. It's terribly dangerous to stray from the group. If you get lost down here, you might never find your way back."

You follow Louis through the winding tunnels. It's rough and slippery. You almost fall once. It's also chilly.

"I wish I'd brought a jacket," Tonya whispers. You agree. The sun may be shining above ground, but it's damp and cool down here.

"We're about to enter the ossuary," Louis says as you come upon a large chamber.

Turn the page.

The words *Arrête! C'est ici l'empire de la mort* are written above the entrance. Louis tells you it means, "Stop! Here lies the Empire of the Dead."

The ossuary takes your breath away. It's filled with bones. Piles of bones. Walls of bones. Thousands of neatly stacked skulls stare blankly at you.

The ossuary was officially named the Paris Municipal Ossuary in 1786.

Tonya grabs your arm. "This is creepy," she whispers.

It *is* creepy. *These were once people*, you think. And now their remains are being used as decorations. A part of you feels like it's wrong even to be here. But you can't look away.

"Look over here!" says one of the other tourists, a young woman named Sonja. She's found a tunnel that's blocked off. "It says we're not supposed to go this way, but I see a light down there!"

She's right. There's a soft, glowing light flickering from somewhere down the tunnel. The passageway is gated off, but the gate is not securely closed.

Turn the page.

You look around. Louis and the rest of the group are a little farther down in the tunnels. Louis is busy answering questions and not paying any attention to you. It would be easy to slip through and take a quick peek.

"Don't even think about it," Tonya says, biting her nails. "There's no way I'm going down there."

You grin. "I know you won't. But there's nothing stopping me."

Tonya shakes her head. "Are you crazy? There's plenty to see here without sneaking off. Let's just head back to the rest of the group."

To return to the group, turn to page 59.
To check out the blocked-off tunnel, turn to page 60.

"Show us what you found," you say, heading left. The tunnel forks off again and again, but Ines knows exactly where to go.

"When you've been down here enough, you get a good sense of direction," she says.

Puddles of water—some of them ankle-deep—cover the way. René laughs as Tonya carefully steps around them. "Don't bother," he says. "You're in the catacombs. You're going to get wet."

He's right. The air is damp and musty. The sound of dripping water is everywhere. Your shoes squish on the rock floor as you creep along. Even though you try to be careful where you step, your pants are soon soaked up to your knees.

Soon you come to a spot where the tunnel widens. "Check this out," Peter says, shining his light on one of the walls.

Turn the page.

You gasp. It's a painting! Life-sized skeletons and spirits adorn the walls. They're bright and vivid, captured forever by spray paint. You've seen hundreds of paintings already on your trip, but this one holds your eye in a new way.

"Creepy," Tonya says. She doesn't share your appreciation for the graffiti art.

The catacombs have their own "cave police" called cataflics. Their role is to protect and preserve the catacombs.

"We don't condone graffiti in the catacombs," René explains. "Cataphiles are supposed to keep them as they are. But it is cool, isn't it?"

Just then you hear a low groaning followed by a crunching sound.

"What was that?" Tonya asks.

Peter, René, and Ines look concerned. "That sounded like something collapsed," Ines says. "It doesn't happen often, but it does happen."

"Collapsed?" Tonya gasps. "I don't like the sound of that. We should turn around!"

René scoffs. "You two do what you want. The exit is straight down that way. We're going deeper."

To head back to the exit, turn to page 54.
To continue on your adventure, turn to page 56.

There's no question about what you want to do.

"Where's the fun without the adventure?" you ask. Ines gives you a big grin and leads the group down the passageway to the right.

But as the minutes tick by, all you see is more tunnel. "Everything looks the same," you say, disappointed.

"That's the danger," René answers. He holds up his phone. "And that's why these maps are so important. So many of these tunnels look the same. One wrong turn and you might never find your way out."

The tunnel has taken a sharp downward slope. The air smells damp.

"Look," Tonya says, shining her light ahead.

The tunnel floor dips into a black pool. To your surprise, Peter steps in. The dropoff is sharp. He is quickly knee-deep in the water. He turns and gives the group a smile.

"Good news, everyone," Peter says. "It looks like we get to take a swim!"

"You've got to be kidding me," Tonya says.

"It's all part of exploring," Peter replies. Ines is already putting everyone's phones into a waterproof pouch.

"Look," Peter says, pulling out a headlamp and putting it on. "Feel free to go back if you want. Otherwise, get ready to get wet."

You stare at the dark water. Was this really what you had in mind?

To return to the exit, turn to page 54.
To step into the water, turn to page 58.

"Sorry guys," you say. "I think this is as far as we go. Thanks for bringing us, but Tonya and I need to be heading back."

Ines gives you a concerned look. "Are you sure you can make it back on your own?"

You glance over your shoulder. It was a pretty straight shot. You don't think it'll be any problem getting back to the manhole. "We've got it," you say. "Don't worry."

She shrugs. "Well, nice to meet you. Enjoy the rest of your trip."

You watch and the three of them disappear around a corner. Their lights slowly dim, and then fade away. You and Tonya are alone. The realization sends a chill up your spine.

"Let's get out of here," you say. You make your way through the tunnel, retracing your steps. Soon, you come to a fork. Tonya starts down one tunnel while you move for another.

"Wait a second," she says. "It was this one."

"No, it was that one," you insist. You shine your lights down both passageways, but both just lead into darkness.

"Look," you say, sighing. "We can't be far from the exit now. Why don't we each go a little way down the tunnel we think is the right one. If we see the exit, we'll shout."

Tonya makes a face. "Split up? Is that really a good idea?"

To agree with Tonya and stay together, turn to page 63.
To split up and search for the exit, turn to page 65.

"Well, if you're not worried, then I'm not either," you say. "Let's keep going."

As you move deeper into the maze of tunnels, you get a greater sense of the age and size of the catacombs. You try to imagine what it must have been like for those who built them so long ago.

Few changes have been made to the catacombs since they opened to the public in 1809.

The ceiling looms closer and closer. You can touch it with the palms of your hands in some places.

"What's this?" René says, coming to a stop. He shines his light on a pile of broken stone. "This wasn't here last time."

"Maybe this was the noise we heard," Tonya says.

Peter scratches his head. "I guess so. Interesting. Collapses in the catacombs are rare, but they do occur."

René moves his light up to the tunnel's ceiling. There's a thin, jagged crack. A cloud of dust slowly seeps out of the crack.

"We should get out of here," Tonya whimpers.

To look closer at the crack, turn to page 72.

To run, turn to page 74.

You've come this far. Why stop now? You hand your phone to Ines for safekeeping. Then you follow Peter into the water. The cold water almost takes your breath away.

You swim until you hit a wall. "Now what?" you ask. "We can't go any farther."

René smiles. "The tunnel probably rises ahead. If it didn't, there wouldn't be water here. Let's see if we can make it to the other side."

With a deep breath, you dive under the water and start to swim. You keep a hand on the wall as you go, not wanting to lose your bearings. You count as you swim . . . *20 . . . 21 . . . 22*. There's no end in sight. Panic starts to set in. You keep counting . . . *30 . . . 31 . . . 32*. You can't go much farther. You're going to need air!

To turn around, turn to page 68.
To press on ahead, turn to page 70.

You give the tunnel one last look, then shrug your shoulders. "You're right, Tonya," you say. "We'll just stick with the tour."

You spend the rest of the afternoon glued to Louis's side. He tells the group how old the catacombs are and how they became a mass grave in the late 1700s. The skulls start to seem almost friendly.

Too soon, you're back up to the surface. You're a little disappointed, knowing that you only saw a tiny fraction of what lies beneath the ancient city. But then your stomach rumbles. You and Tonya head off to your next adventure—to try a Parisian crepe. Soon, your very safe and ordinary trip into the catacombs is just another memory of Paris. Maybe you'll return one day.

THE END

To follow another path, turn to page 9.
To learn more about the Paris Catacombs, turn to page 103.

You still regret not going with Ines and the other cataphiles.

"Sorry, I just want to take a quick look," you say. Tonya stares at you with a scowl on her face.

You slide through the gate and make your way down the corridor. It's narrow here. You have to walk with your shoulders slanted forward just so you don't scrape against the rough walls.

The light ahead is dim, but it's definitely there. It grows brighter as you get closer. It's a solid light with a slight blue cast. It captures your attention—so much so that you stumble over a crack in the corridor's floor. Your body lurches forward, but you catch yourself before you fall. You take a deep breath in relief. That was close. You can see how easily someone could fall and get hurt down here.

You make your way around a slight bend in the corridor. Suddenly you see the source of the light. It's a flashlight resting on the corridor floor. Its cone of light illuminates a shape—it's a young woman. She's lying on the ground. For a moment you fear she's dead. Dried blood mats her hair and face. But as you peer at her face, you can see that she's breathing.

The single public entrance to the catacombs is in Paris's 14th district.

Turn the page.

"Hello," you say gently, touching her arm. She stirs and opens her eyes. Her gaze is glassy.

"Help," she says in a raspy voice. "I . . . I fell."

You waste no time running back into the ossuary. You spot Louis and call out for him. He springs into action, calling for help. Soon, emergency teams arrive with a stretcher.

"She'll be OK," says one of the EMTs. "She's lucky you found her though. If she'd been down there overnight, who knows what would have happened. This is why people should never wander off alone into the catacombs."

He's right. It was a bad idea to stray from the group. But for the woman's sake, you're sure glad that you did.

THE END

To follow another path, turn to page 9.
To learn more about the Paris Catacombs, turn to page 103.

Tonya has always had a better sense of direction. One time you actually got lost inside an art museum trying to find the bathroom. Maybe it's best just to trust her. "Fine, lead the way," you say with a huff.

The two of you continue your careful crawl along the passageway. Your feet are soaked and you're shivering. You've never wanted to see the sky as much as you do now.

You're starting to feel crushed. The walls seem very, very close. Panic is setting in. "We're not going to find it!" you shout. "Help! Help! Someone help us!"

Tonya grabs you. "Stop it!" she shouts. "Look!" she points straight ahead. You can barely see it. A glow. Your eyes widen. It's daylight!

Turn the page.

You hurry along toward the light. As the two of you emerge from the catacombs, you feel the weight has been lifted off of your shoulders. You breathe deeply.

Your adventure in the Paris Catacombs is over. You don't think you'll go underground any time soon.

THE END

To follow another path, turn to page 9.
To learn more about the Paris Catacombs, turn to page 103.

"It's not really splitting up," you say. "I mean, it's just for a minute. See if you can spot anything. Then we'll both come right back here."

Tonya reluctantly agrees. She starts down her passageway as you make your way slowly down yours.

"See," you shout. "We can even talk to each other as we go."

"What?" she calls back. You can barely make out what she's saying. It's more of an echo.

It's just for a minute, you remind yourself again. You keep moving, sweeping your flashlight back and forth as you move. You scan for any light ahead, but you can't make out anything.

"How am I supposed to see daylight with this flashlight on?" you mutter to yourself. You click off the light for a better look.

Turn the page.

Darkness seems to drop around you like a heavy veil. Sounds seem louder and farther away. Even though you can't see the walls, they seem closer than ever. There's not a hint of light in any direction. You turn around, searching for any glow. But there's nothing.

You reach toward your pocket for your flashlight. You fumble for it, and it falls to the ground. You can hear the crack of plastic breaking. You drop to all fours, pawing the damp floor. Finally, you find the flashlight. Just by feel, you know it's beyond repair.

Panicked, you rise to your feet. You don't know which direction you're facing. Which direction leads back to Tonya? You're confused. You can barely move.

"Help! Help! Help!" you shout. But the only sound you can hear is your own voice echoing back at you.

Go back the way I came, you think. You're not sure if what's behind you is the right way. But you can't just stand there. As you turn, your foot catches a crack in the floor. You wave your arms, trying to catch yourself as you fall, but it's no use. Your head hits the ground with a thud.

When you wake up, you have no idea how much time has passed. Has it been a minute? Has it been hours? There's no way to know. You're lost and alone. Will Tonya find you down here? Or will the Catacombs of Paris add one more set of bones to their countless millions?

THE END

To follow another path, turn to page 9.
To learn more about the Paris Catacombs, turn to page 103.

You can't risk going farther. You flip yourself around and start kicking back in the direction you came. But you're swimming blind. You swim headfirst into a wall. You flip again, kicking for all you're worth . . . *52 . . . 53 . . . 54.*

BAM! You slam into another wall. You can feel the tunnel's ceiling above you. There's no way to get air. Your lungs are burning. You want to scream, but you know you can't. If you open your mouth, water will rush into your lungs.

Suddenly something grabs your ankle. It pulls you, dragging your body along the ceiling. Just when you can't hold your breath any longer, you're out. You gasp for air as Tonya helps you out of the water.

"You were thrashing all around," she says. "I had to pull you back!"

You throw your arms around your sister. "You saved my life!" you say.

A few moments later, René's head pops out of the water. "We found the way through," he says. "Come on!"

"No thanks," you say, wringing out your shirt. "We've had our adventure for today. You guys go ahead. We're headed back to the exit. Thanks for everything."

Part of you will always wish you'd seen what was on the other side. It's a lifelong regret. But mostly, you're just glad to have escaped the catacombs of Paris with your life.

THE END

To follow another path, turn to page 9.
To learn more about the Paris Catacombs, turn to page 103.

Just a little farther, you tell yourself. You push forward, keeping a hand on the wall. You keep counting . . . *43 . . . 44 . . . 45.*

Suddenly, you're through. You take a deep breath. Tonya pops up behind you a second later. René, Peter, and Ines are hollering and giving each other high-fives.

"What's going on?" you ask. "Did I miss something?"

"This is completely unmapped!" Peter says, waving his phone in the air. "There's no record of this area being explored before. It's possible we're the first people to stand in this tunnel in more than a thousand years! Can you imagine?"

Ines takes careful measurements of the tunnel on her phone as Peter snaps pictures.

"OK," Ines says. "Time to go back."

Some tunnels are sealed with concrete. This stabilizes the ground above and also keeps out explorers.

"But aren't we going to explore more?" you ask.

Peter puts a hand on your shoulder. "We have to record this before we go deeper. It's a major find. We can't risk getting lost down here. Then no one would ever know about this new network of passages."

"Maybe you can come back with us tomorrow," Ines says, smiling.

You can hardly wait.

THE END

To follow another path, turn to page 9.
To learn more about the Paris Catacombs, turn to page 103.

"That's strange," you say. You rub your fingertips along the edges of the crack. "Is it normal for the tunnel to be . . ."

A huge chunk of ceiling comes off in your hand. Bits of debris crumble off, falling down your shirt sleeves and bouncing off your face. You try to wipe the dust away from your eyes. As you lean over, another piece of ceiling hits you in the back of the head.

The ceilings in some areas are very low.

Tonya pulls you to safety. Your eyes clear just in time to see a massive wall of stone collapse, blocking your exit.

But that's not the worst news. As you explore your surroundings, you find an even larger pile of broken stone blocking the path ahead. You are trapped. Your light is running out. Cell phones get no reception down here. And although the cataphiles insist that people know they've gone into the tunnels, there's no way anyone knows exactly where you are.

Your adventure into the Catacombs of Paris will not have a happy ending.

THE END

To follow another path, turn to page 9.
To learn more about the Paris Catacombs, turn to page 103.

"Run!" you shout. Without a moment's hesitation, you all turn and dart back the way you came. The group's shouting and footsteps are quickly drowned out by a thunderous boom that fills the tunnel. It's caving in!

Plumes of dust shoot through the stale air as countless tons of rock come crashing down. You can feel the rush of air from the falling debris. But you're lucky. You manage to stay just ahead of it. You run, and you don't stop running until the cave-in is far behind you. The five of you finally come to a stop, huffing for air as you lean against the tunnel walls.

"That . . . that was too close," Ines says, shaking. The rest of you are quick to agree. "We have to get out of here in case there's more. Everyone, follow me."

You follow Ines as she quickly navigates back to the surface. When you finally poke your head out into daylight, you breathe easy for the first time since the collapse. The five of you sink down onto the ground and begin to laugh.

Your adventure into the catacombs will be one you never forget. As you look back on it, you realize it was a terrible, reckless idea to venture down there without a guide. But the memories—and friends—you made will last a lifetime.

THE END

To follow another path, turn to page 9.
To learn more about the Paris Catacombs, turn to page 103.

Chapter 4

TO THE RESCUE

It's a relaxing afternoon in Paris. You're sitting in a cafe, enjoying a coffee and watching the people of the city walk by. You've got nothing planned for the day. It's a rare chance to relax, and you're going to take full advantage of it. Everything is setting up for the perfect afternoon.

That is, until your friend Pierre shows up. His face is bright red, and he's breathing heavily.

"What's wrong, Pierre?" you ask.

He takes a moment to catch his breath. "We have a problem," he says. "Ines and some tourists are missing. They went down into the catacombs a few hours ago. We haven't heard from them since."

Turn the page.

Your heart immediately starts pounding. Pierre's news is shocking. Ines is a fellow cataphile. You're a small, tight-knit community who shares a common interest. You delve down into the Catacombs of Paris to map and explore the city's underground tunnels—even the ones that are off limits to the public.

You've been in the caves with Ines many times before. She's smart and careful. If she hasn't checked in, that means there's something wrong.

"Let's go," you say. "I'll need to stop for my gear."

Pierre shakes his head and lifts a backpack. "There's no time. I've got everything we need. I know where she was exploring yesterday. The entrance isn't far from here."

You and Pierre weave through the bustling streets. He veers off into a series of little-used alleyways and heads to a manhole. The manhole cover is moved to the side.

"That's got to be where they went in," Pierre tells you.

The two of you put on your gear. Despite the warm weather, you slip into a light jacket—the underground catacombs can be chilly. You lace up a pair of waterproof boots. You check the two flashlights Pierre hands you. One is your primary light and one is a backup. You never, ever go into the catacombs without a backup light.

"Let's go," Pierre says.

Usually, trips below ground come with a sense of fun and adventure. Not today. Today, you're all business. Ines might need your help.

Turn the page.

The two of you lower yourselves down the manhole using a series of rungs built into the concrete. After a short climb, you drop down into the catacombs. Your feet hit the stone floor with a plop and a splash. It's been raining, which means that everything will be damp and slick.

Exploring the catacombs outside of a tour has been illegal since 1955.

You move down a straight passageway. After a short walk, it forks in two directions. You shine your light into both tunnels. You don't see any signs telling you which way Ines went. Cataphiles take pride in leaving no traces behind. Preserving the catacombs is one of the most important parts of what you do.

"Which way do we go?" Pierre asks. "Should we split up?"

Normally, you'd reject splitting up. It's dangerous to venture alone into the catacombs. But this is an emergency. Every second counts. Is it OK to do it, just this once?

To stay together and choose a passageway, turn to page 82.
To split up and cover more ground, turn to page 85.

You quickly dismiss the idea of splitting up. "No, we can't do that," you say. "The last thing we need is two more people in need of rescue. If we're going to do this, we do it right. We do it safely."

"I've never used this entrance before," Pierre says. "Have you?"

"No," you answer. "I just found out about it from Ines a few days ago. I wonder if it links up to the entrance the police sealed off a few months ago."

Your group is always on the lookout for new ways to access the catacombs. The police seal any new entrances as soon as they can. That's why most cataphiles are so tight-lipped about where they can get in. And it's why you were surprised to hear that Ines was bringing a couple of outsiders in with her.

Some of the tunnel walls are covered in graffiti. You frown at it. The brightly colored spray paint ruins the mysterious atmosphere of the catacombs. You pass an intersection littered with soda cans and candy-bar wrappers. Teenagers like to come down here to party sometimes. Their litter makes you even angrier. Without even thinking about it, you pick up the trash. You will throw it away later.

You work your way through a narrow passage. In some places, it's so tight that you have to walk sideways to squeeze through.

"What's that?" Pierre asks. He points his beam of light at a pile of loose rocks lying on the tunnel floor ahead. You just shrug your shoulders. You're in a mine. Piles of rocks aren't unexpected.

Turn the page.

As you continue, though, you see more and more rubble on the floor. Down here, there's no telling if it's been there a day or a century. But something seems unsettled.

That's when you hear a groaning noise. It sounds like rock scraping against rock.

"What was that?" Pierre asks.

"Whatever it is, it can't be good," you reply. "I'm not sure we should be down here."

"But if something's wrong, Ines needs us more than ever," Pierre argues.

To continue on, turn to page 89.
To turn back and head for the surface, turn to page 98.

Time could be critical. You need to cover as much ground as you can. You bend your safety rules just this once. "You go that way," you say, pointing to the right. "I'll go this way. Be safe."

At one point, there were 300 known entrances to the catacombs. Many have been sealed, but new doors are being opened all the time.

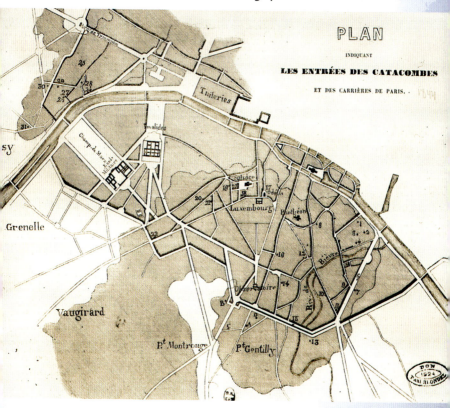

PLAN

INDIQUANT

LES ENTRÉES DES CATACOMBES

ET DES CARRIÈRES DE PARIS.

Turn the page.

You watch as Pierre's light disappears down the passageway. Then, with a deep breath, you head the opposite direction. You've never gone into the catacombs alone before.

The tunnel narrows. Soon it's so tight that you have to walk with your shoulders at an angle. When the tunnel finally opens up again, you're met with a solid rock wall. It's a dead end!

Or is it? Before you turn around, you notice a small opening near the floor. You might be able to squeeze through. Ines definitely could have.

To turn around, go to page 87.
To try to squeeze through the opening, turn to page 91.

You might be able to fit through the opening, but it would be a big risk. It's better to turn around and check in with Pierre.

You've always felt comfortable in the catacombs. But now, alone, you feel uneasy. A quick glance at your watch shows you that you've been down here for half an hour. You've got another 30 minutes or so of battery left in your primary flashlight. Once that's gone, you'll only have your backup. You'll have to head back to the surface. You don't want to be caught down here in the dark.

Your boot slips on the wet, slick tunnel floor. You fall fast and hard. As you flail your arms, your flashlight flies out of your hand. It hits the floor just a second after you do. The light blinks and dies.

Turn the page.

You groan, rubbing your head and backside. Everything hurts. With your light out, the catacombs are pitch black. You sit there for a moment in the darkness with your head throbbing.

What's that? Did you hear something? You strain to listen. Was it a voice? It's so faint that you could have imagined it.

You reach into your pocket and grab your backup flashlight. Could Ines be calling for help?

To head back to meet Pierre, turn to page 94.

To search for the noise deeper in the catacombs, turn to page 96.

Pierre is right. Time is critical. You need to keep going as fast and as safely as you can.

The passageway dips, leading you deeper and deeper into the catacombs. "Would Ines have gone this far?" Pierre asks.

You've known Ines for years. She's a good explorer, but she's a bit reckless. You sigh.

Turn the page.

The average temperature in the catacombs is 57 degrees Fahrenheit (14 degrees Celsius.)

"Yes," you say. "She might have. Let's look for another five minutes. If we don't find anything, we'll head back."

You don't need five minutes though. The tunnel before you has collapsed. A massive pile of jagged rock blocks your way.

"Wow," Pierre says. "I've never seen a collapse like this before. It looks recent."

Now what do you do?

To give up the search and turn around, turn to page 98.

To try to get past the rubble, turn to page 100.

"Ines!" you shout. "If you're there, I'm coming!"

The opening is just big enough to fit through. You lie flat on the wet tunnel floor and go feet first through the rectangular opening. You push your legs through, then force your torso. Finally, you raise your arms over your head and give a strong push, hoping to feel the tunnel open on the other side.

But that doesn't happen. Instead, the opening narrows sharply. It feels as if part of the stone above you has collapsed.

"No!" you shout. Now you'll never be able to make it through. You'll just have to go back the way you came and continue your search somewhere else. You push off your feet to go back through the opening.

Turn the page.

But you don't move. Your boot is caught in a crack. You pull. You wiggle your foot. No luck. You try to pry your foot free of the boot. Nothing works—it's wedged too tight. You feel cold sweat on your face. The more you struggle, the more trapped you feel.

The skeleton of Death guides tourists through the Paris Catacombs in a print made in 1816.

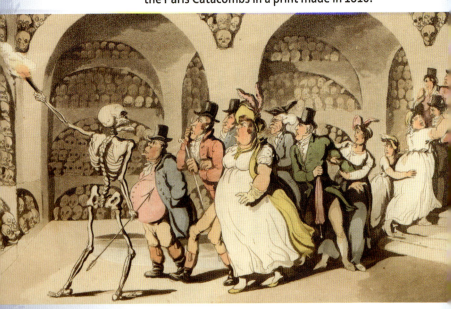

"Help!" you cry. "Heeeeeeelp!"

The minutes tick by. Your flashlight dims, sputters, and then finally dies. You can't reach your backup light in your pocket. It wouldn't do you any good if you could. You're trapped.

You can only hope Pierre calls the police for help. It's what you should have done in the first place.

THE END

To follow another path, turn to page 9.
To learn more about the Paris Catacombs, turn to page 103.

You take a long look back down the tunnel. You can't hear anything now. It could have been your imagination. The darkness, along with a knock on the head, could leave anyone hearing things.

"No," you say out loud, hoping that the sound will reassure you. "I've got to head back."

You pick yourself up. Your pants are soaked from the wet tunnel floor. You're cold, sore, and still just a bit woozy from the fall. You put your hand on the tunnel wall to steady yourself as you head back.

You keep your eyes and ears open the rest of the way. You don't see any sign of Ines and her group. You have little trouble navigating your way back to the exit. You've spent enough time down here. You wait until Pierre returns.

"No luck?" you ask. He shakes his head. You sigh. You don't have much choice now. "Let's go up," you say. "We'll call the police. They've got dogs trained to sniff out survivors. They'll have a far better chance finding Ines than we do."

You try to sound hopeful. But you know the truth. When someone is lost in the catacombs of Paris, there's a real chance he or she will never be found.

THE END

To follow another path, turn to page 9.
To learn more about the Paris Catacombs, turn to page 103.

Your head is swimming from the fall. You know that you're in no condition to go deeper into the catacombs. But you thought you heard something, and you have to be sure.

As you head deeper into the tunnel, you pause to listen. You think you hear the voice again. Or was it just dripping water? You have to know. You press on, deeper and deeper. You come to an intersection. Someone has spray-painted a skull and crossbones on the tunnel walls.

Vandals, you think, annoyed. They're the reason these parts of the catacombs are off limits. It doesn't occur to you that the painting could mean anything else. As you go deeper, your light begins to flicker. That means you've been down here for almost an hour.

"Just a little farther," you whisper to yourself. You beg your flashlight to hold out.

The flashlight begins to dim, but it doesn't go out. It does do a poor job of showing you the way, though. As you hurry on, you don't see that the tunnel leads to one of the large wells that falls straight down into the quarries. One moment you're trotting along through the passageway. The next, you're falling! You bounce off of sharp, jagged rocks.

The landing will not be soft. You know that the Paris Catacombs has claimed one more soul.

THE END

To follow another path, turn to page 9.
To learn more about the Paris Catacombs, turn to page 103.

You don't like this. You sweep your flashlight back and forth. Dust is heavy in the air. Down here in the catacombs, dust tends to settle. If it's in the air, that means it's recent. And from the sounds you just heard, you're afraid the ceiling could collapse at any moment. Even a loud noise could cause a cave-in.

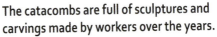

The catacombs are full of sculptures and carvings made by workers over the years.

"We've got to get out of here," you whisper. Pierre takes a long, hard look, but he has no choice but to agree. The two of you turn around and hurry back to the surface. As you emerge into the light of day, you feel a heavy weight on your shoulders. You will call the authorities in hopes they can find your friend. But you can't shake the feeling that when you left the catacombs, you were also saying goodbye.

THE END

To follow another path, turn to page 9.
To learn more about the Paris Catacombs, turn to page 103.

Every instinct tells you to run. But you can't bring yourself to leave. What if Ines is on the other side of the rubble?

"Ines!" you shout. "Ines!"

Silence. Pierre's breathing is the only sound you can hear. Then you hear it. A muffled voice, soft and distant. "Help! We're trapped!"

You look at Pierre. His eyes are wide.

"Ines!" you shout together. "We're coming!"

You start moving the pile of rubble out of the way. The stone is heavy, and it takes both of you to move the biggest pieces. Thirty minutes pass. Then an hour. Your primary flashlights dim and die. You work by the glow of Pierre's backup light, saving your own for the journey back up.

Finally, you break through. Pierre's light shines through a small opening to the other side. "We're here!" he calls. "Just hold on!"

You paw at the opening until it's large enough to crawl through. You help pull Ines and four others through. They've got cuts and bruises, and they're covered in dust, but otherwise they're OK. You wrap Ines up in a big bear hug.

"I thought we were dead," Ines says, sobbing.

"You're not," you answer. "But we all will be if we don't get moving. We're down to one flashlight."

It's a frantic trip back to the surface, but you make it. Daylight has never looked so good.

THE END

To follow another path, turn to page 9.
To learn more about the Paris Catacombs, turn to page 103.

Chapter 5

EMPIRE OF THE DEAD

Few places in the world are filled with as much wonder—and terror—than the Paris Catacombs. It's a maze of more than 200 miles (322 kilometers) of underground passageways that travel far beneath the city streets. The tunnels, which were dug for mining limestone, are at least one thousand years old.

It wasn't until the late 1700s that the catacombs earned their nickname: The Empire of the Dead. At the time, Paris was facing a crisis. The city's graveyards were overfilled. Old graves were being dug up to make room for the newly dead. Bones were stacked on top of each other inside the cemetery walls.

In 1780 heavy rains caused one of the city's main cemetery walls to collapse. Corpses spilled out onto the streets. Something had to be done.

Paris did not have to look far to find a place for its dead. The ancient quarries and tunnels underneath the city seemed like the perfect final resting place for more than 6 million people. It was a massive effort to dig up and move the bodies. It started in 1785 and continued on and off until about 1814. Many of the bones laid there are arranged in ornate patterns, decorating walls and columns.

Since then, the Paris Catacombs have remained a curiosity to some and a fascination to others. They opened for public viewing in 1874. The tunnels have hosted explorers, filmmakers, ghost hunters, thieves, and soldiers. Today, firefighters use them to practice rescue missions.

Bones are arranged based on the cemetery they came from.

The bones in the ossuary were arranged as a way to bring in tourists. It worked. The first people to explore with a guide arrived in 1967. Since then, hundreds of thousands of visitors come to admire the walls famously lined with skulls and bones.

The catacombs have given rise to the strange culture of the cataphiles. These enthusiasts delve into the depths of the catacombs, exploring and mapping the seemingly endless network of tunnels and ossuaries. Their work is illegal but also important.

Exploring in the dark isn't without risk. Pits, mine shafts, and wells—with and without water—can all be found in the tunnels. And not all the water is clean or safe. Although many paths have been mapped and recorded, others remain a mystery.

It's little surprise that the catacombs have claimed their share of victims. One wrong turn can leave an explorer hopelessly lost. One missed step can lead to a disastrous fall. One stroke of bad luck can leave explorers trapped alone in the dark. The catacombs are a strange and dangerous place, but they're also full of wonder.

TRUE STORIES OF THE PARIS CATACOMBS

1783: Philibert Aspairt, the doorman at a Paris hospital, entered the catacombs. Legend says he was searching for a treasure trove of wine hidden in the tunnels. He was not found until 1804, and by that time it was too late. The ring of keys on his belt was the only thing left to identify. He was just a few steps away from an exit.

1939–1945: During World War II, German troops occupied Paris. Some citizens formed a secret resistance to the enemy German army. Resistance fighters often used the catacombs to move around the city and avoid German detection.

2004: Police found a small cinema set up in one of the catacombs' off-limits chambers. There were carved stone benches for 30 people and included a bar, restaurant, private rooms, and a bathroom. When authorities returned a few days later, the cinema was gone. All they found was a note that read, "Do not try [to] find us."

2016: Thirty-year-old Alison Teal of Hawaii brought her surfboard into the flooded chambers of the catacombs. Teal became the first person to surf through the world's largest grave.

2017: Thieves made their way through the catacombs to pull off a stunning heist. From the depths of the catacombs, they drilled into a wine cellar and stole about 300 bottles of high-priced, vintage wine.

2017: Two teenage boys wandered into the catacombs. They quickly became lost. They survived three days in darkness, suffering from hypothermia, or low body temperature. Rescue workers and dogs found the boys and brought them safely to the surface.

OTHER PATHS TO EXPLORE

◆ Many people look at the ossuaries as a work of art, with their carefully arranged skulls and other bones. But some argue that each of those bones represents a real person, and that using their remains in art is disrespectful. How might you feel if you knew someone would one day use your bones in art? Would you be OK with it?

◆ Cataphiles have formed their own society that centers on the catacombs. They are very secretive. Some don't even use their real names while underground. How might a cataphile feel about outsiders coming to the secret tunnels that they love?

◆ The citizens of Paris faced a crisis in the late 1700s. They had nowhere to bury their dead. As bodies stacked up, it became a health crisis. Eventually, workers brought the bodies underground at night. Why do you think they did this? As a citizen of Paris, would you have objected to the work being done during the day? Why or why not?

READ MORE

Hyde, Natalie. *Ancient Underground Structures.* Underground Worlds. St. Catharines, Ontario; New York: Crabtree Publishing, 2019.

Roza, Greg. *Ossuaries and Charnel Houses.* Digging Up the Dead. New York: Gareth Stevens Publishing, 2015.

Winterbottom, Julie. *Frightlopedia: An Encyclopedia of Everything Scary, Creepy, and Spine-chilling, from Arachnids to Zombies.* New York: Workman Publishing, 2016.

INTERNET SITES

The Catacombs of Paris
https://www.cometoparis.com/paris-guide/paris-monuments/the-catacombs-of-paris-s955

The Paris Catacombs
http://www.catacombes.paris.fr/en

The Unbelievable Story of the Paris Catacombs
https://www.walksofitaly.com/blog/paris/paris-catacombs

INDEX